Shannon  **contact.**

Sex with him had been amazing. She never would have guessed that they would have hit it off in bed the way they had.

Finally he looked at her. "We need to talk about what happened."

Boy, howdy, did they.

"I'm sorry, Shannon." He grimaced. "I accept full blame—" his gaze cut to the bed "—for what happened."

Sorry? Swell—just what every girl yearned to hear the morning after.

She snatched her clothes from his hand. He might act as though making love hadn't been a big deal— but they both knew they'd set the sheets on fire.

"Seems like just yesterday I was bandaging your knees and wiping your runny nose."

"You're only nine years older than me." Obviously their age difference bothered him.

"Old enough to know better." Gaze glued to the tips of his boots, Johnny walked to the door. "Like I said, I'm sorry. Good luck at the rodeo. Drive safe."

Then he was gone.

Dear Reader,

Welcome back to Stagecoach, Arizona! *The Cowboy Next Door* is the first story in my new six-book series for Harlequin American Romance. You may recall meeting Dixie's brothers in *A Cowboy's Duty* (August 2012). The Cash brothers were named after country-and-western legends by their deceased mother, whose lifelong search for her true love left each of her sons with a different father.

I love writing about the dynamics of family relationships and the drama that results in family members interfering in each other's lives. In my new series, I'll explore how growing up without a father has impacted the choices in life that each of the Cash brothers has made and the consequences of those choices.

As the firstborn son, Johnny grew up taking care of his siblings and has been accused on more than one occasion of acting more like a parent than a brother. Being overprotective of his siblings comes naturally to Johnny, but when a run-in with his sister's best friend, Shannon Douglas, triggers lusty thoughts, he's not sure what to do. Shannon doesn't have a problem with their age difference—her issue with Johnny is that he thinks he can still tell her what to do, and she rebels when he tries to interfere with her goal of winning a national rodeo title. I hope you enjoy reading how Johnny and Shannon struggle to overcome the baggage from their childhoods and find their way as a couple.

I love to keep in touch with my readers. Email me at marin@marinthomas.com, and follow me on Facebook and Twitter. Visit www.marinthomas.com for more information on my books.

Happy Ever After…The Cowboy Way!

Marin

The Cowboy Next Door

MARIN THOMAS

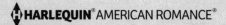

Recycling programs
for this product may
not exist in your area.

ISBN-13: 978-0-373-75463-2

THE COWBOY NEXT DOOR

Copyright © 2013 by Brenda Smith-Beagley

Printed in U.S.A.

ABOUT THE AUTHOR

Marin Thomas grew up in Janesville, Wisconsin. She left the Midwest to attend college in Tucson, Arizona, where she earned a B.A. in radio-TV. Following graduation she married her college sweetheart in a five-minute ceremony at the historic Little Chapel of the West in Las Vegas, Nevada. Over the years she and her family have lived in seven different states, but they've now come full circle and returned to Arizona, where the rugged desert and breathtaking sunsets provide plenty of inspiration for Marin's cowboy books.

Books by Marin Thomas

HARLEQUIN AMERICAN ROMANCE

*The McKade Brothers
**Hearts of Appalachia
***Rodeo Rebels

To my agent Paige Wheeler of Folio Literary Management: thank you for your expert guidance the past ten years and for helping me achieve a longtime dream of becoming a Harlequin author. Here's to the next decade and wherever my writing takes us!

Chapter One

On a hot, mid-August Saturday Johnny Cash stood in the cowboy ready area of the Butterfield Stage Days Parade and Rodeo in Gila Bend, Arizona, and watched the fireworks display between lady bull rider Shannon Douglas and all-around rodeo cowboy C. J. Rodriguez.

The hand-gesturing and boot-stomping drew a lot of notice and Johnny edged closer, ready to intervene if the argument quickly went south.

"You're supposed to be my man, not Veronica's," Shannon said.

No surprise that the notorious buckle bunny Veronica Patriot had sunk her claws into another cowboy. The woman was hell on boot heels and took what she wanted—mostly cowboys in committed relationships. If that was the case, and Rodriguez had cheated on Shannon, then Johnny felt bad for her.

Shannon was his sister's best friend and Johnny had known her most of his life. Nine years her senior, he'd been a big brother to the little girl who'd spent countless afternoons playing at the Cash pecan farm or trailing after him at her father's spread where Johnny worked as a seasonal ranch hand.

Rodriguez jabbed his finger in the air. "I can't help it if I attract women everywhere I go."

Hands fisted, Shannon stood her ground. "You're ticked off that I won last week."

"You didn't beat me." Rodriguez glanced at his competitors, who pretended not to listen.

Shannon laughed. "You're sore because fans are finding out you're not the superstar you claim to be."

The feuding couples' audience showed no signs of intervening. Pretty soon the rodeo officials and cameramen would notice the confrontation playing out behind the chutes and broadcast the lovers' spat on the JumboTron.

"Shannon." Johnny stepped from the shadows and touched a finger to the brim of his black cattleman's Stetson.

She flashed him a grateful smile.

"Well, if it ain't the Man in Black." Rodriguez snickered.

Johnny's hackles rose. What the hell had his mother been thinking when she'd named him and his brothers after country-and-western singers? It had been bad enough that they'd all been fathered by different men. From the day Johnny entered kindergarten, he'd been teased—not that his mother had cared.

When his biological father, Charlie Smith, had split after Johnny's birth, Aimee Cash had become an absentee mom, gallivanting across the Southwest, searching for the next Mr. Right. She hadn't been there when Johnny had come home from school with his first black eye—Grandma Ada had hugged him and insisted there was room in the world for two Johnny Cashes. Eventually he might have learned to turn the other cheek, but every year or two, another brother had been born and saddled with a moniker that needed defending until he grew old enough to fight his own battles. And Johnny had made his fair share of trips to the principal's office during his school career.

"Back off, Rodriguez." He leveled a sober stare at the cowboy.

"This is bullshit." Rodriguez threw his gear bag over his shoulder and stomped off. The onlookers dispersed.

"You okay?" he asked Shannon.

"Yeah. C.J.'s just frustrated with his riding, that's all." She rolled a clump of dirt beneath her boot.

Johnny noticed she wore Dynasty Boots. He glanced at her gear bag—that, too, sported the Dynasty Boots logo. The last he'd heard, Wrangler Jeans was promoting Shannon and Rodriguez's cross-country tour, highlighting women's bull riding. He motioned to the boot stitched on her shirt. "I thought Wrangler sponsored you."

"They did." She watched the rodeo helpers load a bull into a nearby chute. "Dynasty Boots offered me and C.J. a better deal and bought out our contract with Wrangler."

"What kind of better deal?"

"If C.J. and I continue to compete against each other and keep up our sham of a romance—fans love that we're a couple—" she said, rolling her eyes "—we—"

"You're not a couple?"

"Not anymore." She shrugged. "Anyway, whoever has the most wins after the Tucson rodeo in January earns a fifty-thousand-dollar bonus."

Johnny whistled between his teeth. "Where does the score stand between you two?"

"Dead even."

"No kidding?"

"Did you think because C.J.'s a man he'd be ahead of me in the competition?"

"No…I…" Johnny shrugged. In truth, he believed bull riding was best left to cow*boys,* but if there was ever a cow*girl* who could go the distance with the men, Shannon Douglas was that girl.

"If I want to win the title of Cowgirl of the Year, I need to beat C.J." She shifted her weight from one foot to the other, clearly agitated. The hotshot cowboy had rattled her.

"You sure you're okay?" His gaze roamed over her body.

"Why are you looking at me like that?"

"Rodriguez must be blind."

Her cheeks flushed pink. Even though Shannon was a tomboy, the subtle signs of a pretty woman were evident. Her turbulent green eyes, fringed with thick black lashes, glowed with a vibrant, determined spirit. Then there was her mouth, plump lips that begged a man to… Startled by his train of thought, he cleared his throat. What the heck was he doing—cataloging his sister's friend's body parts? At least he'd stopped before he'd checked out her—

"I got to the rodeo late. Did you ride this afternoon?" she asked.

"Sandpiper tossed me on my keister."

"Did any of your brothers compete?"

"The rest of the gang stayed behind to work on the bunkhouse."

"I heard Dixie threw all of you out of the farmhouse after she and Gavin married."

"You heard right." He nodded at C.J. "Was that your normal warm-up routine?"

"Hardly."

"Ladies and gentlemen, we're about to kick off the men's bull riding event, but first, we have a special treat for you." Applause and whistles filled the arena. When the noise died down, the announcer continued. "Shannon Douglas is about to show us that cowgirls are as tough as cowboys when it comes to bull riding!"

The crowd noise was deafening. Johnny had no idea Shannon had become so popular on the circuit. "You sure you're okay?" She shot him a dark look, so he said, "Good luck," and moved aside. He didn't stray far—in case Rodriguez got it in his head to pick another fight with her. After she put on her Kevlar vest, protective face mask and riding glove, she climbed the chute rails while the announcer finished his spiel.

"Shannon Douglas hails from the Triple D Ranch near Stagecoach. She's been competing in roughstock events since high school and you won't find a tougher cowgirl in the whole state of Arizona!" The JumboTron displayed a close-up of her as she waved to the fans. "This cowgirl's about to tangle with Boomerang, a veteran bull known for his tight spins."

Shannon stretched a leg over the bull and settled onto his back. She wrapped then rewrapped the rope around her gloved hand and Johnny worried that she was thinking about her quarrel with Rodriguez.

He spotted her partner inching toward the chute and stepped into the man's path. He wasn't letting the rodeo playboy taunt Shannon. Only after the gate opened and Boomerang sprang free, did Johnny turn to the action inside the arena.

Shannon hung on through three spins. As the seconds ticked off the clock, the bullfighters moved into position, ready to help if needed.

Six…seven…

The buzzer sounded and Shannon waited for an opening to dismount. Boomerang chose for her. The bull kicked out at the same time he twisted his back end and she catapulted through the air. She hit the ground and skidded several feet across the dirt. His heart stalled when Boomerang turned on Shannon as she struggled to stand.

Head down, the bull charged and a collective gasp rippled through the stands. The bullfighters made a valiant attempt to intervene, but the beast was fixated on his rider.

Move, Shannon, move!

She must have felt the ground shake, because she rolled sideways in the nick of time and the bull's horns missed her by inches. Scrambling to her feet, she stumbled toward the rails as the rodeo helpers guided Boomerang to the bull pen.

When Shannon's boot hit the bottom rung, Johnny held out his hand and her green eyes flashed with relief. Adrenaline pumped through his blood and he yanked her too hard over the rails, her momentum carrying him backward. They tumbled to the ground in a tangle of arms and legs, Shannon sprawled on top of him. Damned if he couldn't feel the soft mounds of her breasts through her Kevlar vest. His arms tightened around her and the first thought that popped into his head was how good she felt pressed against him.

"There you have it, folks!" the announcer bellowed. "Shannon Douglas has bested Boomerang!"

The announcer's voice startled them and Shannon rolled off of Johnny. Another cowboy offered his hand and helped her to her feet. Her competitors congratulated her with fist pumps, high fives and hearty pats on the back. By the time Johnny stood, she was no longer smiling. A few yards away, dressed in a red-and-white-checked cowgirl blouse, Veronica Patriot hung on Rodriguez like a cloth over a picnic table. Obviously the cowboy wasn't trying very hard to play up the romance between him and Shannon.

"Hey, Johnny." Andy Kramer, a bareback rider, stopped by his side and nodded to Shannon as she removed her protective gear. "Bet you're glad Dixie quit riding bulls."

For sure. Last summer Shannon had convinced Johnny's sister to compete in a few rodeos, but Dixie had turned up pregnant after the second one and scratched her final ride.

"You wanna grab a beer when we leave here?" Andy asked.

"Sorry, I've got a date." He planned to stop at his girlfriend's apartment and surprise her with a night on the town. He hadn't seen Charlene in forever and the last time they'd talked on the phone, the conversation had been strained. He hated that they were growing apart, but he'd been forced to put their relationship on the back burner the past year in order to deal with family problems and the pecan farm's financial crisis.

"See ya at the next go-round." Andy walked off.

Johnny grabbed his gear and strolled over to Shannon, intending to say goodbye, but Rodriguez beat him to her.

"Can we talk somewhere?" Rodriguez nodded to the stands.

Shannon caught Johnny's eye and he asked, "Want me to stay?"

"Thanks, I'm good."

After she left with Rodriguez, Johnny headed for the

exit. What the hell had gotten into him? It was one thing to look out for Shannon at the rodeo—another to hold her close when they'd crashed to the ground.

Cool off, buddy. No harm done.

Then why had X-rated thoughts drifted through his mind when Shannon had been sprawled on top of him?

He cut through the rows of pickups to his truck parked at the rear of the lot. Once he stowed his gear, he drove south toward Stagecoach. In an effort to put Shannon out of his mind, he listened to talk radio. Ten miles passed and he hadn't heard a word the radio host said. Johnny pulled off at the next roadside gas station and bought a coffee in the convenience store, then sat in the truck and stared out the windshield.

When had he stopped loving Charlene?

He couldn't recall the last time Charlene and the word *love* had occurred in the same thought. Johnny's memory floated back in time…first one month…then two…then six and finally a year. He couldn't blame the demise of his and Charlene's relationship all on his siblings and the farm. His feelings for his longtime girlfriend had been gradually fading, but because he'd been comfortable with the status quo, he'd paid no attention to the signs.

He and Charlene had been together a little over seven years and he hadn't asked her to marry him. The last time she'd brought up marriage, he'd recently found out Dixie was pregnant and then he'd gotten word the agricultural company leasing the pecan groves had gone bankrupt. Marrying Charlene would have added another person to his list of responsibilities.

Unbeknownst to his brothers, Johnny had made the mortgage payment on the farm for the past eight months, depleting his savings—funds that had been earmarked for a house once he and Charlene tied the knot.

Shannon. When she'd landed on top of him this afternoon, he'd felt a sharp stab of arousal shoot through his body. He hadn't experienced a physical zap like that with Charlene in forever. He sipped his coffee and winced as the scalding liquid burned his tongue. If anything good had come out of running into Shannon at the rodeo, it was recognizing that tonight he had to end his relationship with Charlene. She deserved better than to be strung along.

He started the truck and merged onto the highway. An hour later, he took the exit for Yuma. He arrived at Charlene's complex and parked in a visitor spot, then removed her apartment key from his key ring.

When he rounded the corner of the building, he bumped into a man. "Sorry." Together they ascended the stairs to the second story where the guy stopped in front of Charlene's apartment and rang the bell.

Stunned, Johnny gaped at the man's dress slacks and polished wing tips.

The door opened and Charlene smiled. When she caught sight of Johnny, her eyes widened.

"Hello, darlin'," Johnny said. The color drained from her face and he thought she might cry. "Mind if I have a word with you in private?"

She motioned for Mr. Businessman to enter the apartment, then stepped onto the landing and shut the door. "I can explain."

"How long have you been seeing him?"

"This is our second date." She sighed. "I was going to tell you the next time I saw you, but we haven't spoken in three weeks."

Had it been that long? "Don't apologize." His pride hurt that she'd moved on before they'd officially broken up, but in the grand scheme of things, he was relieved she was making this easy for him.

"I'm sorry, Johnny. I should have told you I wasn't happy."

She'd given off plenty of clues that her feelings for him had changed, but he'd been too distracted to notice.

After he handed her the apartment key, she said, "Wait here." She returned a few minutes later—hair mussed. Obviously the new guy wanted him to know he'd staked his claim on Charlene.

She held out a cardboard box filled with his toiletries and personal items. "If you'd like, I can fetch the two necklaces and pair of earrings you bought me."

They'd been together seven years and that's all he'd given her? "Those were gifts. I don't want them back." He shifted the box in his arms. "Good luck with—" He nodded to the door.

"Sean. We met at work." Charlene kissed his cheek. "You'll always be special to me, Johnny."

"Take care," he said.

The apartment door closed and the scraping sound of the dead bolt ended their seven-year relationship.

Johnny left the complex feeling as if an enormous weight had been lifted from his shoulders. He'd had good times with Charlene and she'd been the first woman he'd fallen in love with, but happy-ever-after hadn't been in the cards for them.

Once he reached his truck, he decided he didn't feel like being alone. He'd stop at a bar and properly mourn the end of his relationship with Charlene. She'd stuck it out with him for longer than most women would have, and the least he could do was drink a few beers and pretend she'd broken his heart.

SHANNON ENTERED THE WHISKEY River Saloon—not because she wanted a beer, but because she hoped to find C.J. in the midst of all the rowdy cowboys and buckle bunnies. She needed to talk sense into her *partner* before his actions jeopardized everything she'd worked so hard for.

She hated the strain between her and C.J., but if he didn't rein in his wild ways and pretend they were a couple in public, she'd lose her shot at a national title. Both her brothers and her father had won rodeo titles and she was determined to win one, too.

If only she hadn't fallen victim to C.J.'s charm when they'd first hit the road together, but she'd been no match for the womanizing cowboy and had stupidly believed he'd remain faithful to her after they made love. She'd learned her lesson the hard way when the very next day C.J. flirted with a rodeo groupie right in front of her. Whatever romantic feelings she once carried for him had died a quick death, which made acting like a lovesick couple all the more difficult.

She really didn't care if he slept with other women, as long as he kept his liaisons private. If fans believed their romance was a big lie, ticket sales might plummet, then Dynasty Boots would pull their sponsorship—and there went her shot at the title.

"You here alone?"

Shannon felt the whisper of a breath near her ear. She spun and came face-to-face with Johnny Cash. "I'll buy you a beer," he said.

"I could use one, thanks."

"Comin' right up."

Shannon watched Johnny saunter over to the bar, admiring the snug fit of his jeans. When he came back with their drinks, he motioned to a table on the other side of the dance floor. Once they were seated, she had trouble keeping her eyes off his face. Why had she never noticed how sexy his chiseled jaw was before now? "How's Dixie?"

"She and Gavin are trying for another baby."

Poor Dixie. She'd suffered a miscarriage last fall and although the pregnancy hadn't been planned, she'd been devastated. "I hope everything goes well this time."

A stilted silence grew between them and Shannon squirmed in her chair. Since when had she ever had trouble talking to Johnny? "I'm sorry you had to witness the spat between C.J. and me." She picked at the label on the beer bottle and made a pile of confetti on the table. When she chanced a glance at Johnny, he was grinning. "What?"

"Like I said before, Rodriguez is a fool." He saluted her with his beer, then took a swig.

Shannon fought a smile. Johnny had always made her feel better when she'd been down in the dumps. "Speaking of relationships, are you still with Sherry…Cheryl—"

"Charlene. We broke up."

"I'm sorry. Dixie never said anything."

"She doesn't know yet."

"So your breakup with Charlene is fairly recent?"

"You could say that, but we've been growing apart for a while." He nodded to the crowded floor. "Care to dance?"

"Sure." Shannon wasn't in any hurry to go to the motel room and sleep, only to be jarred awake in the middle of the night from the headboard banging against the wall in the room next to hers as C.J. and his latest buckle bunny went at it.

Johnny held out his hand and she threaded her fingers through his, finding his callused grip comforting. He pulled her close and they swayed to the music, his six-foot-one frame towering over her five feet six inches. For as long as she'd known Johnny he'd made her feel safe.

"Where does Mack's band play?" she asked.

"What?" Johnny bent his head, moving his ear close to her mouth.

She caught a whiff of cologne and breathed deeply. "I asked where Mack and his band performed." Someone nudged Shannon from behind and her mouth bumped Johnny's cheek. A tingling sensation spread through her lips.

He swung her away from the exuberant dance couple. "The Cowboy Rebels play the bars in Stagecoach."

Before Shannon replied, a voice from behind her spoke. "Thanks for leaving me stranded at the rodeo."

Her feet stopped moving and Johnny's fingers tightened against her back as he swung her to face C.J.

"I assumed one of your bunnies would give you a ride into Yuma," she said.

"You've got a lot of nerve complaining about me being with other women when you're chasing after your own cowboys." C.J. glared at Johnny.

She pulled her hand free from Johnny's and said, "Can you give us a minute?"

After Johnny left the dance floor, C.J. twirled her between the other couples. "I want you to stop flirting with women at the rodeos," she said.

"Jealous?"

"Hardly." She snorted. "You're not going to ruin my chances at a national title because you can't stick to the script and pretend we're a couple."

"You really think you can beat me in Tucson?"

"Damn straight." Her answer made him laugh.

"If you don't keep your love interests out of the public eye, the fans will catch on that our romance is made-up and neither of us will win anything because Dynasty Boots will break our contract."

C.J.'s expression sobered. "Okay, I'll tell the ladies they have to sit in the bleachers with all the other fans."

"And make sure you don't leave the arena with any of your bunnies. Meet up with them somewhere else."

"Same goes for you and the 'Boy Named Sue.'" He nodded to Johnny.

C.J. could be a real ass sometimes, but she let his sarcasm slide. If not for the night he'd gotten drunk when they'd first hit the road together and spilled his guts about his traumatic childhood, she might never have fallen for him. Like her, he'd been raised by a single father until he was nine and his father was sent to prison for killing C.J.'s mother. C.J. spent the next several years shuffling between foster homes until he ran away at the age of fifteen. Rodeo was C.J.'s family and like most families there were some siblings you got along with and others you didn't. For whatever reason, the Cash clan rubbed C.J. the wrong way.

"Johnny's like a big brother to me. Nothing's going to happen between us."

"He didn't act like a big brother earlier today."

"Do we have a deal then?" She didn't want to discuss Johnny.

"I'll try my best." He offered a cocky bow, then sauntered out of the bar.

"Ready for another beer?" Johnny asked a moment later.

Why not? It had been a long time since she'd let her hair down and enjoyed a few dances with a handsome cowboy—even if the cowboy happened to be her best friend's brother.

Chapter Two

"One more dance," Shannon whispered in Johnny's ear.

Once Rodriguez had left the bar, Shannon had insisted on dancing up a storm—so much for mourning his breakup with Charlene. The band had left an hour ago and now oldies but goodies played on the jukebox. "How many beers have you had tonight?" he asked.

"Three." She wiggled closer, her hips rubbing the front of his jeans with just enough friction to start a riot behind the zipper.

He'd done an admirable job pretending she didn't arouse him, but each song they danced to, he found it more difficult to remember that Shannon was his sister's best friend and the boss's daughter. Time to end the torment. He took her hand and guided her toward the exit.

"Well, damn." The curse floated from Shannon's mouth as soon as they stepped outside the Whiskey River Saloon.

Johnny surveyed the dark parking lot. "What's the matter?"

"He took off with the truck."

"Who?"

"C.J. took the truck Dynasty Boots loaned us while we're traveling the circuit." She teetered toward Johnny.

"Whoa." He steadied her and escorted her to his pickup. "I'll give you a lift home." He was glad Rodriguez had left Shannon stranded at the bar. She was in no shape to drive and she'd have put up a stink if he'd taken the keys from her.

"Not back to the ranch," she said when he opened the passenger-side door. "C.J. and I have rooms at the Hacienda Motel in Yuma. We're leaving early in the morning for California." She fumbled with the seat belt and he helped her snap the buckle into place before hopping in on the driver's side.

The drive to the motel took fifteen minutes, and Johnny parked in the back then walked her to the room. After two failed attempts to swipe the key card in the lock, he opened the door for her and flipped on the lights. "What about your things?" he asked.

"They're in the truck with C.J." She sank onto the end of the bed and tugged off her boots.

Johnny checked the bathroom for boogeymen and made sure the window was locked. When he faced Shannon, she wore only a black lace bra and matching panties. *Wow.* There was nothing little girl about her underwear and her body was sexy as hell—her athleticism evident in her toned arms, sinewy thighs and six-pack abs.

"You better catch some sleep," he mumbled, averting his eyes. When he made a move for the door, she stepped in his path. Their gazes locked. Her green eyes glinted with desire as she licked her lips. The air in the room evaporated, leaving him light-headed. He'd seen Shannon lick plenty of things through the years—Popsicles, suckers and Oreo cookie cream, but never had he watched her roll her tongue across her lower lip and stare at him as if he were a big juicy steak.

She reached for his shirt and ripped the snaps open. The rush of cool air hitting his chest hardened his nipples. Then her hands fumbled with his belt as she pressed her mouth against his and kissed him.

The brush of her lips coincided with the soft bump of her lace-covered breasts against his chest, triggering a rush of testosterone through his bloodstream. He let her deepen the kiss, confident in his ability to stop her in a second…maybe a minute…maybe never.

His shirt ended up on the floor, and then her hand slipped inside his jeans. He meant to move away, but instead, he trapped her fingers against him and thrust his tongue inside her mouth. She moaned but broke off the kiss and walked to the bathroom, where she stopped in the doorway and crooked her finger.

For a split second he considered making a break for the door, but then the next thing he knew he was standing in the middle of the bathroom and Shannon was tugging his boots off and pushing his jeans down his legs. Her bra and panties joined his clothes on the floor before they stepped under the spray of warm water, made all the hotter by the heat radiating off his skin. She soaped his body, each caress driving him closer to the edge. Then it was his turn, and he made sure every inch of her was sparkling clean.

After rinsing off, they toweled each other dry and kissed their way back to the bed, where she collapsed onto the mattress and he sprawled across her.

"My wallet's on the floor in the bathroom." He nibbled her breast before leaving her to retrieve a condom.

When he returned, Shannon lay on the bed like a bewitching siren, her damp hair spread across the pillow, her green eyes beckoning. His last sane thought as he sheathed himself was how surreal the moment felt and that he hoped he'd never wake up from this fantasy.

JOHNNY WOKE TO the feel of Shannon snuggled against his side. He took shallow breaths and lay motionless—afraid to wake her. Afraid to confront what had just happened.

The morning sun peeked through the one-inch gap between the drapes and the air conditioner—illuminating the room enough that he could see Shannon's face. He swallowed hard. With her eyes closed and her mouth slightly open, she looked younger than her twenty-four years.

What in the hell had he done?

He closed his eyes and silently cursed.

She's practically your sister.

Last night Shannon hadn't behaved like a little sister and he hadn't behaved like a big brother. What was the matter with him? He should have been looking out for her, not taking advantage of her.

She's too young for you.

Nine years separated them. She might be younger, but she seemed older—maybe because she'd grown up in an all-male household and had learned to be tough and independent practically from birth. If their age difference wasn't enough to convince him to leave her alone then the fact that her father had hired him as the new foreman of the Triple D should be reason enough to keep his hands to himself.

He couldn't afford to screw up his job with Shannon's father. He needed the steady income to pay the mortgage on the farm until he found an agricultural company to lease the orchards. The pecan grove had been in the family four generations and losing the land would cause Johnny's grandfather to roll over in his grave. As his mother's firstborn, he'd experienced a special bond with his grandfather—the old man had offered a guiding hand when Johnny's own father had wanted nothing to do with raising him. Johnny would do everything in his power to ensure the farm remained in the family.

Shannon stretched lazily against his side, her fingers caressing his groin. A shock, strong enough to jump-start his heart, raced through his body. He should grab his clothes and split, but someone had to be the grown-up this morning.

Before he talked himself into making love to her for a third time, he rolled off the mattress and escaped to the bathroom, where he took a cold shower and dressed in yesterday's clothes. When he stepped into the bedroom, Shannon was sitting up against the headboard, the sheet tucked beneath her arms—thank God. Telling her that what they'd shared had been a mistake would be impossible if he had to stare at her naked breasts.

Shannon waited for Johnny to make eye contact. Sex with him had been amazing. She never would have guessed that she and Dixie's brother would have hit it off in bed the way they had.

Finally he looked at her. "We need to talk about what happened," he said.

Boy, howdy, did they. She glanced at the clock on the nightstand, then silently cursed and leaped from the bed, dragging the sheet with her. "C.J. and I have to leave in fifteen minutes," she said, shutting the bathroom door in Johnny's face.

She made quick use of the facilities then, realizing her clothes were in the other room, she wrapped the sheet around her and opened the door. Johnny stood by the window holding her bra and panties.

"I'm sorry, Shannon." He grimaced. "I accept full blame—" his gaze cut to the bed "—for what happened."

Sorry? Swell, just what every girl yearns to hear the morning after.

She snatched her lingerie from his hand. He might act like making love hadn't been a big deal—but they both knew they'd set the sheets on fire. Even though she'd been with only three guys—Johnny being one of them—their lovemaking was unlike anything she'd experienced before, and she knew he'd enjoyed it, because he'd been pretty darn vocal.

He spun when she dropped the sheet to put on her panties. "Seems like just yesterday I was bandaging your knees and wiping your runny nose."

"You're nine years my senior. So what?" Obviously their age difference bothered him.

"Old enough to know better."

"I'm decent now."

"Like I said, I'm sorry." Gaze glued to the tips of his boots, Johnny walked to the door. "Good luck at the rodeo. Drive safe."

Then he was gone.

Tears burned her eyes, but she held them at bay and blamed her wishy-washy emotions on too little sleep. After she tugged on her boots, she carried the truck keys and her cell phone outside to see if C.J. had come back to the motel or spent the night somewhere else.

Johnny's truck was gone from its parking spot—he'd wasted no time making a getaway. She shielded her eyes from the sun and scanned the rows of vehicles. There in the back sat the familiar black Dodge with the big red-

and-yellow boot painted on the door. While she waited for C.J. she might as well phone her father—maybe it would take her mind off of Johnny.

Shannon cut through the lot toward the truck and punched the number 7 on her speed dial. "Hey, Dad, did I catch you at a bad time?"

"No, I'm on my way to the barn."

Good. Short phone calls were best between them.

"I won yesterday in Gila Bend."

"Congratulations," he said.

As much as Shannon loved her father, just once she'd like to hear excitement in his voice when they talked about her rodeo career. She knew he didn't believe women should ride bulls—neither did her brothers, but she'd been competing in roughstock events since high school and that's what she knew how to do best.

"I'm getting closer to winning that title, Dad. I can almost taste it." Her father had been a National Champion in bareback riding and both her brothers had won rodeo titles—Luke in bull riding and Matt in team roping. National titles were in the Douglas DNA and Shannon intended to earn one herself.

"You comin' home soon?" he asked.

"C.J. and I are traveling to California, but we'll be back at the end of the month to compete in Yuma. Maybe you can come watch me." Silence greeted her suggestion.

What happened to the man who'd praised her when she'd been a little girl beating out the boys in all the mutton bustin' competitions? Back then, her father hadn't cared that she acted like a boy. Then one day she woke up with breasts and suddenly he insisted she quit rodeo.

Time to change the subject. "How are things at the ranch?"

"Might have a buyer for Cinnamon."

After her mother had walked out on the family when Shannon was three, her father had focused his energy on growing his cutting horse operation. Now that her brothers were busy with their law practice in Yuma and she traveled the circuit all year, most of the horse training fell on his shoulders.

"Is Roger excited about retiring?" The foreman had worked at the ranch for over three decades. This past year, he'd fallen and broken his hip, requiring a hip-replacement operation. Her father had finally convinced the seventy-five-year-old man that it was time to put away the branding iron.

"You know Roger. He doesn't have a whole lot to say," her father said.

Maybe not, but Shannon bet the ranch hand looked forward to spending time with his sister in Florida. "Have you hired anyone to take his place?" Aside from raising cutting horses her father ran a small herd of cattle on the property—more than enough work to keep two men busy.

"Johnny Cash."

Shannon sucked in a quiet breath. Why hadn't Johnny told her he was the new foreman? No wonder he'd beat a hasty retreat this morning. He was probably worried how her father would react if he found out about their tryst.

"Johnny's not starting until Roger clears his things out in a couple of weeks."

"That's great."

The motel door opened and C.J. stepped outside in a pair of black boxers and white tube socks. When he spotted her, he waved.

"Gotta go, Dad."

"Good luck in California."

The words weren't heartfelt, but Shannon gave her father credit for saying them. "I love you" dangled on the tip of her tongue, but instead she said, "Call you soon." She shoved the phone into her jeans pocket.

"Who you talkin' to?" C.J. asked.

"Nobody." As she stared at his muscular chest and bulging biceps, an image of Johnny's leaner athletic build flashed before her eyes. If viewing a man's naked chest was all it took to trigger the memory of her and Johnny's lovemaking, then she was in big trouble, because cowboys were always changing their shirts behind the chutes.

She checked the time on her cell phone. Eight o'clock. "We've got to be at the fairgrounds in Glendale by one-thirty." Glendale, California, was four and a half hours away. "I'm leaving in ten minutes with or without you." She got into the truck and started it, then adjusted the air conditioner to cool down the cab.

With less than a minute to spare, C.J. stowed his gear in the backseat. She didn't wait for him to put on his seat belt before peeling away like a bat out of hell.

"You pissed off about Veronica?"

The buckle bunny would be history soon enough, seeing how C.J. blew through women faster than a dust devil bounced across the desert.

When she remained quiet, he said, "I'm gonna try harder to keep my love life private." He tugged on his boots. "Maybe we should ham it up more for the fans."

The last thing she wanted to do in public was act like an idiot over the womanizing cowboy. "Our normal routine has worked fine so far. Why mess with it?" The most she and C.J. had done in front of the cameras was hug and exchange high fives.

"I bet the fans want to see us kiss."

Fat chance. "They'll have to settle for fantasizing about us kissing."

"You're a hard woman, Shannon."

She'd learned from the best—her father. She jacked up the volume on the radio. C.J. leaned his head against the seat, tipped his hat over his face and fell asleep.

At one in the afternoon they pulled into the rodeo grounds west of Glendale. C.J. stretched. "You ready to go down, Douglas?"

The cowboy was about to find out hell hath no fury like a pissed off cowgirl. She pocketed the truck keys then walked off with her gear. Once she signed in for her event, she went to the livestock pens to check out her draw—Dead End.

The bull appeared docile, its tail twitching at the flies buzzing near its rump. The short, muscular bull lifted his head and a shiver raced down her spine. The animal was a machine whose only purpose was to hurt cowboys.

She left the stock pens and reported to the Dynasty Boots tent, which had been set up next to the bleachers. As usual, C.J. was nowhere in sight, leaving her with the responsibility of signing autographs and shaking hands.

"Will you sign this?"

"What's your name?" Shannon asked the little girl who wore a pink cowboy hat.

"Lizzy."

Shannon scribbled her name across the program. "Are you a real cowgirl?"

"Yes."

"Hurry up, Lizzy." An older man waited a few feet away.

"You gonna ride broncs or bulls when you grow up?" She handed the program to the girl.

"Daddy says ladies don't rodeo, but I wanna ride bulls like you."

"Do I look like a lady, Lizzy?"

The girl nodded.

"Do I ride bulls?"

Lizzy nodded again.

"Then I guess your daddy's wrong. Ladies do ride bulls." Shannon winked. As the little girl walked off, Shannon called after her, "Don't ever let anyone tell you what you can or can't be just because you're a girl."

An hour later, she left the booth to prepare for her meeting with Dead End.

"Where've you been?" C.J. asked when she arrived in the cowboy ready area.

"Signing autographs. Where've you been?"

His gaze drifted to the bleachers where a blond-haired buckle bunny watched them. C.J. tipped his hat and the woman blew him a kiss.

At least he'd kept his promise and made the bimbo wait in the stands.

"Get ready to lose," Shannon said. "I drew a better bull."

"It's not about the bull, baby." His smile taunted her. "It's all about the cow...*boy.*"

"Ladies and gentlemen, hold tight to your hats as we kick off our bull riding event!"

Shannon donned her Kevlar vest then put on her face mask and riding glove. She rubbed resin on the leather as rodeo helpers loaded Dead End into the chute.

"Up first this afternoon is talented cowgirl Shannon Douglas." The fans hooted and hollered and a few waved pink posters with Shannon's name on them.

A group of cowboys nearby stared. Most of her competitors welcomed her in the male-dominated sport, but there were a few who felt threatened by her presence.

"Shannon Douglas from Stagecoach, Arizona, is about to battle Dead End, a bull from the Kindle Ranch in Las Cruces, New Mexico. This cowgirl's gonna have her hands full!"

Before approaching the chute, Shannon closed her eyes and pictured herself riding the bull to the buzzer, and then she imagined her dismount—a solid landing before making a break for the rails. Her sponsor didn't care if she won, but Shannon did. She never entered the chute without believing she'd make the buzzer.

Showtime. When she straddled Dead End, the bull balked and attempted to rear so she lifted off his back.

"Looks like Dead End wants nothing to do with Shannon," the announcer said.

The JumboTron showed a close-up of her and the bull. When Dead End became feisty again, forcing her off a second time, a collective gasp rippled through the stands. C.J. grasped her shoulder and whispered, "Thought I'd act like a concerned boyfriend."

"Back away, C.J. You're not helping." She'd ridden her share of uncooperative bulls before, but something felt off about Dead End, and she worried the ride wouldn't go the way she wanted.

Third time's a charm. She eased onto the bull and secured her grip, then nodded to the gate man. Dead End bolted into the arena.

The first kick was powerful and thrust Shannon forward, but she hung on. Then the bull spun, and the arena became one big blur of color before her eyes. The seconds ticked off inside her head...four...five...

Dead End switched directions so quickly that Shannon

didn't have time to adjust and she fell into the well—the inside of the spin. She hit the ground hard, but sprang to her feet and raced for the rails, trusting the bullfighters to intercept Dead End if he gave chase. Helping hands grasped her arms and lifted her to safety.

"There you have it folks, Dead End won that round against Shannon Douglas. Maybe next time, cowgirl."

Back in the cowboy ready area, C.J. said, "I'm taking the lead today." He swatted her backside with his hat and the fans cheered as their interaction was displayed on the JumboTron.

"Folks, all-around cowboy C. J. Rodriguez is up next. As you know, he's traveling the circuit with Shannon." The announcer whistled. "They're a pair of regular bull-ridin' lovebirds."

The audience cheered and it was all Shannon could do to keep smiling when C.J. put his arm over her shoulder and preened for the camera.

Chapter Three

"Your sister's worried about you. You've been MIA for over twenty-four hours."

The last thing Johnny wanted to do was confess his whereabouts the previous night to his brother-in-law. The memories of his rendezvous with Shannon churned his stomach after spending most of today at the Triple D with her father. Talk about uncomfortable—he hadn't even been able to look his boss in the eye when asked if he'd watched Shannon ride at the Gila Bend rodeo.

"'Bout time Dixie worried a little." Johnny climbed the farmhouse steps and strolled to the opposite end of the porch where Gavin Tucker sat on the swing. Leaning a hip against the rail he said, "Now she knows what I went through all those years keeping track of her."

"Must be tough being the eldest," Gavin said.

"At least you took one of my siblings off my hands." From an early age Johnny had felt a sense of responsibility for his siblings. He recalled a middle school psychologist once telling him that he should start acting like a brother instead of father. He'd thought the woman was nuts, but he'd never forgotten that conversation and at times wondered if his need to protect and guide others was rooted in a suppressed desire for his own father to show interest in him.

"You look tired." Johnny guessed nightmares were robbing the former soldier of sleep. Dixie had told him that her husband had been diagnosed with PTSD after he'd served in Afghanistan, and a few mornings when Johnny had left the bunkhouse before dawn he'd found Gavin asleep on the porch swing.

"Did Dixie tell you Shannon Douglas's father offered me the foreman's job at the Triple D?"

"She did. Congratulations. When do you start?"

"Not until the end of the month. I was over there today helping Clive train a cutting horse."

"Are you quitting the rodeo circuit?"

"I'm cutting back on events until I get a handle on running the Triple D."

The squeak of the screen door interrupted the men and Dixie stepped onto the porch. She smiled at Johnny. "I thought I heard your voice." She joined her husband on the swing, curling up against his side. "Did you see Shannon yesterday?"

He wished he could blame his serious lapse of judgment last night on Dixie's insistence he check up on Shannon at the rodeo. But he was a big boy, and no one had forced him to follow the lady bull rider into her motel room.

"Shannon didn't make it to eight on her bull but she's fine." Uncomfortable with the conversation he pushed away from the railing. "I've got a few phone calls to make."

"Wait. The other day you never said whether or not Charlene was moving into the foreman's cabin with you."

He might as well get this over with. "Charlene and I broke up."

Dixie gasped. "What happened? You two have been together forever."

Gavin kissed the top of Dixie's head. "Think I'll grab a bite to eat." He disappeared inside the house.

"You're not leaving until you tell me what happened." Dixie patted the empty spot next to her.

When had his baby sister become so bossy? He sat down. "This feels weird—you listening to my problems." In the past, he played the role of Dear Abby.

"I'm sorry about Charlene." Dixie hugged him.

Through the years Johnny had been the hugger, consoling his siblings when their grandparents had been busy with the farm or their mother had been out of town chasing the next love of her life. Johnny had grown to resent his mother for putting her own wants and needs before her children's and when Aimee Cash had passed away the day before his eighteenth birthday, he hadn't shed a tear. How could he cry for someone he'd barely spent any time with?

"Why did you two break up?" Dixie asked.

He repeated his standard line—because it sounded good. "Charlene and I have been growing apart for a while."

"It's my fault."

"How's that?"

"You were worried about me when I got pregnant last summer, then I miscarried and I was such a mess that you wouldn't leave me alone for a minute."

"It wasn't your fault, Dix. I ignored the writing on the wall." And Shannon had been his wake-up call.

"What do you mean?"

"You put years into a relationship, then one day you look at the other person and wonder what you have in common." And when there's no zip, zap or zing left in the kisses, it's time to say goodbye.

"How's Charlene taking it?"

Pretty damn well. "She'll be fine."

"And you?"

Shannon's face popped into Johnny's mind. What would Dixie say if he told her that he had the hots for her best friend? "I'll be too busy at the Triple D to mope."

"Are you sure you want to move into the foreman's cabin? It's not that far of a drive between the farm and the ranch."

"I'll be back to visit, especially if Gavin's cooking chili for supper."

"Who's going to run herd over the rest of our brothers?"

"It's your turn to keep everyone in line, Dix."

"Gee, thanks."

"If any of them give you trouble let me know and I'll bang a few heads together."

Right then the bunkhouse door flew open and Porter, the youngest brother, stepped outside and ducked as a cereal box flew past his head. "I didn't know you were going to ask her out!" he shouted.

"Looks like you'll be knocking heads sooner rather than later," Dixie said.

"Better see what Porter did this time." Johnny skipped down the steps and cut across the yard to referee the latest fight between his caterwauling brothers.

"THE DOG FOOD is in a plastic bin beneath the kitchen sink." Roger McGee dropped the key to the foreman's cabin into Johnny's hand. The end of August had arrived and with it a changing of the guards at the Triple D.

"I'll make sure Hank gets fed twice a day." Johnny felt bad for the old man as he watched the cowboy struggle to say goodbye to thirty years of his life. If dogs could talk, Hank would say he didn't like his master's departure any more than Roger did. The hound lay in the dirt next to the Ford pickup as if he intended to ride along to Florida.

"Sure you can't take Hank to your sister's?" Johnny asked.

"Animals ain't allowed in the condo units."

"If you ever move into your own place, I'd be happy to drive Hank to Florida."

"That's right nice of you." Roger's eyes glistened as he descended the porch steps. He stopped at Hank's side and patted the dog's head.

Johnny went into the cabin to retrieve the leash, giving the foreman and his dog some privacy. After a minute, he stepped outside and clipped the tether to Hank's collar. The dog refused to budge.

"Best tie him up for a week or two after I'm gone. He might run off."

"Will do." Johnny would have to keep close tabs on Hank. A jaunt through the desert in the August heat might kill the twelve-year-old hound before he reached the highway.

Roger hopped into the truck and gunned the engine. The ranch hand and the boss had said their farewells earlier in the morning, so there would be no big send-off this afternoon.

"Be sure to check in with Clive during your trip." Johnny leaned through the open passenger window and shook Roger's hand a second time. "Take care of your-

self." He'd miss the geezer. Roger had taught him everything he knew about cattle and horses when he'd first
hired on as a part-time wrangler for the ranch fifteen
years ago.

The Ford pulled away and Johnny tightened his grip
on the leash when Hank whined. After a quarter mile,
a dust cloud obscured the truck from view. "Well, boy,
it's you and me now."

Inside the cabin the dog went straight to his bed pillow
in the kitchen corner, where he watched his new master
through sad, droopy eyes. The pathetic stare prompted
Johnny to fetch a Milk-Bone from the cookie jar Roger
left behind, but the dog wanted nothing to do with the
treat. "I'll leave it right here, boy." He set the bone on
the floor. "In case you change your mind."

Johnny stood in the middle of the cabin, facing the
front door. The kitchen sat to his right, the family room
to his left. Behind him was a short hallway with a door
to the bathroom and one to the bedroom. The cabin had
come furnished and included a washer and dryer, dish-
washer, and a full set of cookware, dishes, utensils and
linens. There was also a satellite dish and internet ac-
cess. All he'd had to bring was his clothing, toiletries,
laptop computer and his iPod.

After years of sharing a house with five brothers and
a sister, the quietness of the cabin bothered Johnny, but
he was certain he'd enjoy the solitude once he became
accustomed to living alone. He might as well unpack his
clothes. He made it as far as the hallway when the sound
of horns honking penetrated the cabin walls.

The Cash welcome wagon had arrived.

After making sure Hank remained on his pillow,
Johnny stepped onto the porch and shielded his eyes

from the late-afternoon sun. A wall of dust moved along the horizon as the caravan of pickups drew closer.

His brothers parked helter-skelter in front of the cabin, then got out of their trucks. When Johnny saw them standing in a group, he was reminded again of his mother. All five Cash brothers sported various shades of her blond hair and brown eyes. Johnny and Dixie were the only siblings who shared the same father and they'd inherited Charlie Smith's dark brown hair and blue eyes.

"Hey, Johnny," Willie Nelson, who preferred to be called Will, spoke. "We brought food."

"Did you bring a grill? 'Cause I don't have one," Johnny said.

"Got it covered." Buck Owens walked to the back of his truck and lifted a Weber cooker from the bed. He set it by the porch. "Your housewarming gift."

"Mighty thoughtful of you all." Johnny recognized the dual purpose of the gift—to cook food and to use it as an excuse to drop by unexpectedly for a free meal. Now that Dixie was running her gift shop in Yuma, she rarely put supper on the table for the family. Johnny had done his best to grill a few dinners each week for the group, but now that he'd moved away from the farm, he suspected his brothers were worried they'd starve to death.

"Hey, Mack, what's your housewarming gift for me?" Johnny teased.

Merle Haggard, or Mack, pulled out his guitar. "I'm going to christen this place with a lucky love song." He winked. "Before you know it, you'll have women busting down your door."

Ever since Johnny's brothers had learned about his breakup with Charlene, they'd been concerned he'd sink into a deep depression. Little did they know another woman had already replaced Charlene in his thoughts. He'd had no contact with Shannon since the morning after the rodeo in Gila Bend, but not an hour of the day passed by when she didn't cross his mind.

"I bought you a case of your favorite beer." Conway Twitty set the carton on the porch floor.

"I suppose Isi talked her boss into giving you a deal on that beer," Johnny said.

"Who's Isi?" Porter Wagoner glanced between the brothers.

Conway shot Johnny a dark look, then spoke to their youngest brother. "She's just a friend." Conway used to seek Johnny's advice when he had a dilemma with girls but a while back he confessed that he'd found a new confidant—a waitress at the Border Town Bar & Grill.

"I haven't had a chance to grocery shop. My fridge is empty," Johnny said.

"We got all the fixin's." Will hauled two grocery sacks from the front seat of his truck. "Where should I put this stuff?"

"Inside. Don't let Hank out."

"Roger didn't take Hank with him?" Mack sat on the steps with his guitar.

"No."

Porter and Buck filled the belly of the cooker with charcoal, while Mack strummed his guitar and Conway sang off-key. Johnny went inside to help the second eldest Cash brother with the meal preparations. As much as he'd been hoping to spend the first evening alone in his new digs, he grudgingly admitted that it was nice to know he was missed.

"That dog looks like he's ready to meet his maker in

hound heaven." Will placed the deli containers on the kitchen table.

"Be nice to Hank. He's older than Roger."

"Is Roger taking retirement hard?"

"Yes." Johnny changed the subject. "What's new in your life?"

"Not much since we spoke twelve hours ago." Will chuckled. "What are you gonna do now that you can't boss us around?"

"Just because I'm living at the Triple D doesn't mean I won't be keeping tabs on all of you."

Will's expression sobered. "I can't believe you're the official foreman now."

Neither could Johnny, but he was determined to impress Shannon's father because he needed the job to work out. He hadn't gone to college after graduating high school, and pecan farming wasn't his real passion. He only competed in rodeos to bring in extra money. Working with horses and punching cows was his calling in life.

"Douglas treats his foreman dang good." Will pointed to the fifty-two-inch TV. "Is he charging you rent to live here?"

"No, the furnished cabin comes with the job."

The door opened and Hank rose from his bed ready to bolt. Johnny grabbed his collar. "Whoa, boy." Worried the dog might escape he pushed the bed pillow across the floor and positioned it next to the couch, then tied the end of the leash to a sofa leg.

For the next half hour, the brothers drank beer and talked rodeo on the porch while the brats cooked. "Are you riding in Yuma tomorrow?" Conway asked.

The special event featured only bull riding and chuck wagon races. "I don't think so." But Johnny intended to watch Shannon compete. His big-brother instinct insisted he make sure she was okay after they'd… And there was a part of him, which had nothing to do with brotherly concern, that wanted to find out if the attraction was still there between them, or if what they'd shared two weeks ago had been a fluke.

"What about you?" Johnny asked Conway. His brother rode bulls on occasion but his preference was the saddle back competition.

"I'm heading to Tucson to visit a buddy."

Buck removed the brats from the grill and set the plate on the porch rail while he toasted the buns. "If you get lonely living by yourself, you can always come back to the bunkhouse."

Thanks, but no thanks. As far as bunkhouses went, the one on the farm wasn't bad. They'd installed a bathroom and two window air-conditioning units kept the place cool. Mack had sweet-talked an old girlfriend into selling them a secondhand refrigerator for fifty bucks so there was always cold beer on hand. The place had all the creature comforts except privacy. "I've got it pretty good here," Johnny said.

The matter of his residence resolved, the brothers dug into their food and swapped rodeo stories. Halfway through the meal, Porter brought Hank outside and they all took turns tossing scraps to the hound.

After the meal, Will pulled a deck of cards out of his pocket. "I'm calling the first game," he said. "Acey deucey."

Porter grabbed Hank's leash and the brothers carried the leftover food inside. After the tenth hand of poker, it occurred to Johnny that even though he was ready to move on with his life, his brothers weren't quite ready to cut the apron strings.

"HEY, CLIVE." JOHNNY jogged across the dirt drive and walked into the barn with his boss early Saturday morning. "You plan to go to the rodeo in Yuma this afternoon?"

"Nope."

Clive's curt response startled Johnny. He'd expected his boss to want to see his daughter compete.

"I'd be happy to watch things here if you want to take the afternoon off."

"Got too much work to do." Clive pushed the wheelbarrow through the center of the barn and parked it next to Windjammer's stall.

Fourteen days had passed since he and Shannon had made love and the knot in Johnny's gut hadn't unraveled. "Would you mind if I went to the rodeo?"

Clive grasped a pitchfork and flung clumps of soiled hay into the barrow. "You competing?"

After landing my dream job? "The last thing I need is an injury to prevent me from doing ranch chores."

"Makes no difference to me what you do. You're not officially on the clock till Monday morning."

"Is there anything you want me to tell Shannon?"

The boss wiped his brow. "I don't know what in tarnation I did to make that girl believe riding bulls is acceptable behavior for a lady."

Johnny didn't like the idea of Shannon riding bulls, either, but he felt compelled to defend her. "She's darn good at the sport. It takes courage to do what she does. I'm sure she got that from you."

"Only a matter of time before she gets hurt." Clive spat tobacco juice into the soiled hay.

"I didn't realize you disapproved of Shannon rodeo-ing."

"I didn't mind her keeping up with her brothers when she was a little tyke, but I never thought she'd take bull riding this far. I figured when she grew into a young woman she'd find other interests."

Johnny wished he understood what drove Shannon to compete in the dangerous sport. Maybe the answer was as simple as she enjoyed the challenge. A lot of rodeo cowboys were adrenaline junkies who loved pitting themselves against a bull.

"What did you say to Dixie to convince her to quit riding bulls last summer?" Clive asked.

Evidently Shannon hadn't told her father that Dixie had scratched the final Five Star Rodeo because she'd discovered she was pregnant. Not many people knew that Dixie had miscarried weeks later and Johnny was sure his sister did not want the news to become public knowledge. "Dixie sprained her ankle and couldn't compete." That was the lie his sister had used.

"Why didn't she ride after her ankle healed?"

"She became too busy with her gift shop in Yuma."

"Wish my daughter would find a new hobby."

Hobby? Dixie's Desert Delights was a reputable business that helped support Dixie and her husband.

"Maybe you can talk sense into my daughter."

After their night at the Hacienda Motel, Johnny wasn't sure Shannon cared to speak to him. He'd find out shortly. "If you're sure you don't mind, I'll catch that rodeo in Yuma."

"Makes no difference to me."

"Roger was worried Hank would run off after he left, so I've kept him tied to the porch." He'd given the hound plenty of leash and set extra water and food outside.

"I'll check on him after I'm through here."

"See you later."

Before he reached the barn doors, Clive called his name. "Johnny."

"What?"

"Tell Shannon—" his boss struggled to speak "—to be careful."

"Will do." Johnny jogged to his truck, his chest tightening with anticipation and dread.

THE OUTDOOR ARENA for the Yuma Rodeo Days Ride-off was packed to the gills. Despite the hundred-plus temperature, Shannon smiled for the cameras and signed autographs for young girls who dreamed of becoming lady bull riders. For the past three hours she'd manned the Dynasty Boots booth, waiting for C.J. to take her place. She guessed he'd snuck off—most likely to a horse stall in the livestock barn—with another ditzy buckle bunny. At least he wasn't flirting with women out in the open.

Her sweat-soaked clothes chafed her but the only thing she cared about was winning and evening up the score with C.J., who remained one win ahead. After today's ride, they had a break from competition for two weeks before they traveled to Winslow to compete.

Shannon planned to use the time off to help her father with ranch chores, but that had been before she'd had sex with Johnny. Seeing the cowboy every day and not being able to do anything about her attraction to him would be tougher than riding a rank bull.

"My name's Jenny. Can I have your autograph?" A freckle-faced girl held out a rodeo program.

"You wanna be a cowgirl when you grow up?" Shannon scribbled her name across the cover.

"No, I wanna be like her."

Shannon glanced in the direction the girl pointed and saw C.J. talking to the Yuma Rodeo Days Ride-off queen. The rodeo queen wore fancy boots and a red Western shirt with more rhinestones than stars in the galaxy.

A tug on the program in her hand startled her. "Sorry. Have fun today, Jenny." No sooner had the girl moseyed along than Shannon caught sight of Johnny Cash. She sucked in a quiet breath. Dressed from head to toe in black, he represented his namesake and drew the stares of several women as he walked toward her, his hips rolling from side to side in a confident swagger.

"Hello, Johnny." She resisted pressing her hand against her thudding heart.

His black Stetson dipped. "How've you been?"

That was a loaded question. "Great. I hear you're working for my father."

His gaze locked on the table of programs next to her. "Guess I forgot to mention that."

"Are you settled in at the ranch?"

"Yep." He looked her in the eye. "Your father said to be careful."

"Let me guess. He was too busy with the ranch to come today."

Johnny nodded. "He's worried you'll injure yourself."

She didn't want to discuss her father. "Are you competing?"

"Heck, no." This time his smile was genuine. "I don't want to screw up my gig at the Triple D."

"Be careful what you wish for," she said. "My father can be a demanding man. That's why my brothers traded in their saddles for a library full of law books."

"You ready for today?" he asked.

"Of course." She was always ready—riding bulls was a part of who she was. She checked the time on her cell phone. "I better get going." It was crazy, but instead of making her feel ill at ease, Johnny's presence quieted her jumpy nerves. "Walk with me?"

"Sure."

They strolled through the crowd in silence, Johnny's shoulder bumping hers once—the contact triggering an electric charge, which traveled down her arm and through her fingertips. When they reached the cowboy ready area, he pulled her aside. "What's the matter?"

"What do you mean?"

"You kept looking over your shoulder the whole way here."

"I'm fine." Shannon saw C.J. and stiffened.

"Did you two…get back together?" Johnny's blue gaze intensified. Did her answer matter to him?

"No, we're through."

"Does Dynasty Boots know about the breakup?" he asked.

"No, and we're not planning to tell them." She wished she knew if it bothered him that she and C.J. were pretending to be a couple.

"What bull did you draw?" he asked.

"Heat Miser."

"Heat Miser's a twenty-three-point bull." Left unsaid was the animal's reputation for turning on fallen riders.

Shannon was the first to admit the bull made her nervous, but a draw was a draw and her sponsor paid her to play the game with the big boys. C.J. had drawn Mr. Gigolo, a twenty-one-point bull known for running toward the exit after throwing his rider.

Shannon unzipped her bag and put on her gear.

"Ladies and gentlemen, we're ready to kick off our bull riding event." The announcer's voice boomed over the sound system.

"Don't look now but Rodriguez is heading this way," Johnny said.

When C.J. noticed Johnny, he glared. "What are you doing here, Cash?"

"Making sure you mind your manners."

A cowboy standing nearby snickered and C.J. snapped at Shannon, "You're going down, Douglas."

"Is that any way to talk to your *girlfriend?*" Johnny asked.

C.J. flashed a smug grin.

"Don't let Rodriguez get to you." Johnny grasped Shannon's shoulders. "You've got to keep your head on straight with this bull."

"You're right."

"Ready?"

Whether she was or not didn't matter. It was showtime.

Chapter Four

"Ladies and gentlemen, welcome to the third annual Yuma Rodeo Days Ride-Off!"

The spectators' applause competed with the industrial-sized fans, which moved stagnant air through the building and kept the temperature at a steady eighty-five degrees—not bad considering the thermometer outside hovered at one-hundred-five.

"Yuma is the only town in Arizona to put on a rodeo the last Saturday in the month of August." The crowd noise grew deafening. "This event is for bull riders only, but be sure to stay afterward for the legendary chuck wagon races. Let's have a round of applause for our sponsors, the Yuma Main Street Merchants Association."

Shannon caught C.J. watching her. He wanted her to lose and his steady stare squeezed her like a vise, crushing her chest until she couldn't draw any air into her lungs.

"Take a deep breath and relax." Johnny's quiet voice broke the tension in her body and her lungs opened enough to suck in a gulp of oxygen. "Don't worry about Rodriguez." He grasped her hand. "Concentrate on your ride."

"Folks, we got ourselves fifteen of the toughest rodeo

athletes in the Southwest ready to ride fifteen of the meanest, orneriest bulls on the circuit."

Johnny released her hand, and she resisted the urge to cling to his fingers—leaning on him was a sign of weakness. The only person she could rely on when the chute opened was herself. Gathering her courage, she studied the bulls.

Shannon zeroed in on Heat Miser's rear hooves. Every few seconds the bull kicked the rails, causing Shannon's adrenaline to spike. Her heart rate sped up and her mouth watered—she could taste how much she wanted to even the score with C.J.

Music blasted over the sound system as the JumboTron played clips of bull rides from previous rodeos. "Before our competition begins, let me introduce southern Arizona's famous rodeo couple!" Shannon and C.J. waved to the crowd.

"Shannon Douglas hails from Stagecoach, Arizona, and next to her is our hometown legend C. J. Rodriguez!"

The giant video screen zoomed in on Shannon and C.J., and she forced a smile. C.J. blew kisses at the camera and the women in the stands screamed wildly.

"Sponsored by Dynasty Boots, Shannon and C.J. are traveling the country, promoting women's roughstock events. For those who don't know, Shannon is in the running this year for the prestigious title of Cowgirl of the Year."

When the applause died down, the announcer said, "Place your bets, folks! It's cowgirl against cowboy. Who's gonna come out on top in today's ride-off?"

The crowd went crazy.

Shannon heard several shouts for her name but a whole lot more for C.J.'s. There would always be fans who believed women didn't belong in roughstock events. Most of Shannon's supporters were her competitors who respected talent—female or male made no difference.

"Did you do your research on Heat Miser?" Johnny asked when Shannon dropped back to the ground.

"He kicks twice, spins then kicks again before he comes out of the spin." She'd watched the bull perform at a rodeo in Alamosa, Colorado, which was both helpful and not so helpful. Knowing what she was up against before the gate opened wasn't the least bit reassuring.

"Folks, Rodriguez will ride Gigolo." The announcer chuckled. "Seein' how they're both ladies' men, C.J. and Gigolo ought to get along swell."

Shannon ignored the raucous laughter, tired of the lewd jokes that went hand in hand with her and C.J.'s fake romance. Johnny walked a few feet away to gain a better view of C.J.'s ride.

"It's a fact that Shannon's bull, Heat Miser, is rated higher than C.J.'s, but you can never tell with a bull. Let's see if this cowboy makes it to eight."

C.J. sat on Gigolo's back and made a big production out of fussing with the bull rope, and then the fun began.

The bull's rhythmic bucking pattern—two kicks, a spin then two more kicks—made C.J. look like a superstar. When the buzzer rang he waved his hat at the crowd before dismounting.

Show-off.

C.J. landed on both feet, then faced Shannon's chute and bowed.

"Another stellar ride by one of the best cowboys on the circuit!"

When Johnny appeared at Shannon's side, she said, "Thanks for being here."

"You're ready." He straightened her Kevlar vest and she wished those strong arms would pull her close for a hug. Instead, she gathered strength from the confidence in his voice.

"Don't lean too far forward. Heat Miser is famous for butting heads with his riders."

Mean bulls didn't care for anyone on their backs and it didn't make a bit of difference if the rider was female or male. Shannon adjusted her leather glove, then put one boot on the rail. C.J.'s voice stopped her cold.

"Better hold tight, Douglas, or that bull will stomp your head!"

Shannon placed her boot back on the ground. "Is that any way to treat your better half?" she said, loud enough to turn heads.

Johnny stiffened next to her, but she kept her eyes on C.J. This was part of the show—their love-hate relationship. Dynasty Boots wanted fans to believe they were a warring couple—fiercely competitive during the rodeo then wildly passionate for each other afterward.

C.J. smiled for the cameras. "You'll never make it to eight, Douglas."

Johnny stepped between them. "Give her some breathing room, Rodriguez."

"Jealous, Cash?" C.J. nodded to Johnny's clothes. "I see you're dressing like your namesake."

"You got a problem with my name, Rodriguez?"

"Yeah, it's stupid."

"If you don't have anything nice to say…" Johnny smirked. "You know…shut your mouth."

C.J.'s gaze cut to Shannon. "Is Cash doing all your talking for you now?"

She cringed when she saw their images on the Jumbo-Tron. "Back off, C.J."

"You think I'm afraid of a country-western wannabe?" C.J. puffed out his chest.

Johnny bumped the brim of his Stetson against C.J.'s. "You heard the lady. Back off."

"Make me."

Before Shannon realized Johnny's intent, he swung his fist, catching C.J. across the jaw and knocking him backward. The group of onlookers steadied C.J. before thrusting him toward Johnny.

C.J. threw the next punch, catching Johnny across the cheek, but Johnny kept his balance and took another swing at C.J. The shorter man ducked, then pushed Johnny to the ground, where they rolled in the dirt.

Rodeo officials intervened and pulled the men apart just as the announcer's voice boomed over the sound system. "Looks like there's trouble in paradise."

Cheers and boos echoed through the stands.

Shannon stuck her face in C.J.'s and whispered, "You probably just cost us our sponsorship. Happy now?"

C.J. walked off, rubbing his jaw and the crowd dispersed.

"You okay?" Johnny asked.

"I'm fine." She touched her fingers against the bruise forming on his cheek. "What about you?"

"This isn't the first time I've taken a punch defending my name."

"If you ask me, folks, it looks like we've got ourselves a little love triangle between Shannon Douglas, C. J. Rodriguez and…who's that you say?"

The JumboTron showed the announcer conferring with one of the scorekeepers. "Johnny Cash." The crowd stomped their boots on the metal bleachers. "That's right, folks…the Man in Black."

Johnny escorted Shannon away from the cameras. "Don't worry about anything right now but going out there and sticking like glue to your bull." He winked, then pressed a hard kiss to her mouth. "It's your turn to shine."

Instead of leaving her dazed, Johnny's kiss propelled her toward the chute. Without hesitation she slid onto Heat Miser, but as soon as she grasped the rope, the bull rose on his back legs and Shannon had to scramble for safety.

"Heat Miser's full of hot air this afternoon. Shannon's gonna have her hands full with this bull."

Once Heat Miser stopped protesting, Shannon found her seat and wasted no time wrapping the rope around her hand. She wasn't a fan of suicide wraps and most rodeos didn't allow a rider to tie his glove to the bull rope but this was one time she wished she could use the trick to keep from losing her grip.

After harnessing her anger at C.J. she leaned her shoulder forward and nodded to the gateman. Heat Miser exploded from the chute, his hoof cracking against the gate and sending the rodeo worker diving for cover.

The bull's muscles rippled and clenched as he kicked out. When his hooves hit the ground, the impact reverberated through Shannon's spine and across her shoulders. Clinging to the rope she transferred her center of gravity forward as the bull rolled left. With each second that ticked off the clock, she fought to remain balanced and tuned her ears for the sound of the buzzer.

Just when she believed she'd make it through the ride without Heat Miser throwing his head, the bull dipped, propelling Shannon forward. She tensed, bracing for impact as the bull flung his head sideways. The jolt felt as if someone had swung a baseball bat at her face mask. Dazed, she received a one-second reprieve when Heat Miser planted all four hooves on the ground before gathering his power for another kick.

Face numb, vision blurry, her strength began to ebb. *Hang on…one…more…* The buzzer rang and instinct took over, releasing a final surge of adrenaline as she waited for an opening to dismount.

The bullfighters appeared in her peripheral vision and one of the men shouted at her, but she couldn't hear him through the ringing in her ears. Heat Miser was tiring but even the kick of a tired bull was dangerous. Each time she thought she saw an opening the bull stole it from her. Her arm had grown numb and her vision began to dim. She was running out of time and options. She had to jump.

The last thing she remembered was hitting the ground and the excruciating pain that shot through her left leg before blackness overcame her.

Paralyzed with fear, Johnny was perched on the arena rails, watching the horror unfold before his eyes. Shannon laid facedown in the dirt while the bullfighters attempted to draw Heat Miser away from her. One of the men whacked the bull's butt and the animal gave chase but only for a few yards.

Get up, Shannon. Get up!

She didn't move.

The bull pawed the ground. *Good, God.* Heat Miser intended to freight-train Shannon.

No! No!

Johnny vaulted over the rails and dropped into the

arena. Everything happened in slow motion as he raced toward her body, waving his arms frantically above his head. The bullfighters closed ranks and showed amazing bravery when the bull charged them. One cowboy grabbed a horn but Heat Miser tossed his head, flinging the man through the air like a pesky fly.

A sick feeling gripped Johnny's stomach when he realized he wasn't going to reach Shannon in time. A cowboy on horseback galloped into the arena and attempted to lasso the bull's head but missed his first attempt. There was nothing left between Shannon and Heat Miser but twenty feet of dirt.

Johnny's heart stopped beating when the bull lowered his head and caught Shannon at the waist, hurling her into the air like a rag doll. She hit the ground and rolled several feet before her body came to a stop. Having made his point, Heat Miser trotted off to the livestock pen.

Heart beating like a jackhammer, Johnny skidded to a stop at her side. "Shannon? Can you hear me?"

A bullfighter knelt next to Johnny. "Don't move her. She might have an injury to her neck or spinal cord."

The medics sprinted into the arena ahead of the rescue truck. Johnny held Shannon's hand and whispered in her ear. "You're going to be okay, honey."

"Out of the way!" The paramedic's shout startled Johnny and he scooted over, allowing the medical team room to do their job.

"She's breathing." A medic examined Shannon's limbs and when he touched her left leg, she groaned. "The bone might be broken," he said.

A third medic emerged from the truck with a body board. Once Shannon's neck was immobilized with a foam brace, they rolled her onto the board and strapped her down. Johnny peered through the dented face mask, willing her eyes to open, but they remained closed. "Where are you taking her?"

"Yuma Regional Medical Center."

Johnny waited until they'd loaded her into the truck, then raced through the cowboy ready area as he called Shannon's father on his cell phone. Clive didn't pick up so he left a brief message telling his boss to head to the hospital.

Rodriguez chased after Johnny. "Where are you going, Cash?"

"What do you care?"

"She's not your girl." Rodriguez stopped when they reached the parking lot and Johnny kept walking.

Maybe Shannon wasn't his girl, but she was like a sister to him and right now he was scared to death for her. He jogged to his truck, convinced the tightness in his chest felt a whole lot different from the big-brother pain he experienced with Dixie when she got hurt.

SLOWLY, AS IF someone had thrown a rope over Shannon's head, an invisible force tugged her from blissful darkness into a gray fog. She yearned to see her torturer but her eyes wouldn't open as the voices echoed inside her head.

"Maybe this will convince her to stop riding bulls."

Matt?

"If it doesn't, nothing will."

Luke? Why were her brothers talking about her?

"Do you think she can hear us?"

I can hear you, Dad. Where am I?

"She just moved her hand."

Johnny?

His deep voice calmed her and she no longer cared

that she couldn't open her eyes. As long as Johnny was near, she felt protected. The voices faded for a time until the sound of a throat clearing dragged her from the murky dark back into the gray fog.

"Her leg should be fine."

What happened to her leg?

"Fortunately, the fracture in the tibia was a clean break, but the orthopedic surgeon had to repair a tear in her Achilles tendon, which will require physical therapy after the bone heals."

"What about her concussion?" Matt asked.

"The protective headgear saved her from a more serious blow. She'll have headaches for a few days but there should be no lasting damage."

Listening to the voices exhausted her and her thoughts floated out of reach.

"How long will she have to stay in the hospital?" Clive asked.

"Two days. Three at the most. All of you should go home and rest. She'll sleep through the night, but the nurses will keep an eye on her."

Matt and Luke followed the doctor to the door. "We've got a big trial next week we're preparing for," Luke said.

Tomorrow was Sunday. Johnny assumed Shannon's brothers took at least one day off a week.

"We'll stop by tomorrow night." Matt nodded to Johnny. "See you later."

"I'll take care of things at the ranch if you want to stay here." Johnny spoke to Clive.

"I've got a meeting with a horse buyer first thing in the morning. I'll drop by the hospital afterward." Clive put his cowboy hat on and glanced at his daughter, then shook his head and left the room.

Johnny moved closer to the bed. She looked deathly pale and small beneath the white blanket. He took her hand in his and rubbed his thumb across her knuckles. Guilt pricked him. Had his fight with Rodriguez distracted her and caused her to lose focus? "Damn it, Shannon. You could have been killed today."

He mulled over the past two weeks since he'd run into her at the rodeo in Gila Bend and ended up in a motel room with her. He wasn't able to make sense of his feelings. This burning attraction to her had sprung up out of nowhere.

The room door burst open and Johnny jumped inside his skin, quickly releasing Shannon's hand.

"I got here as soon as I could," Dixie said. "How is she?"

"Concussion and a broken tibia."

"I saw Clive walking through the lobby."

"He's driving back to the ranch tonight."

Dixie approached the bed and arranged Shannon's hair across the pillow. "She's so brave. I never thought she'd get hurt."

Bravery had nothing to do with becoming injured. If you rode bulls long enough, you got hurt—no cowboy or cowgirl was exempt from that rodeo rule.

"Do you think she'll recover in time to compete against C.J. at the Tucson rodeo in January?"

"After almost getting killed this afternoon, Shannon's bull riding days are over."

"Don't underestimate her. She's a lot stronger than you realize." Dixie smiled. "Besides, you can't tell her what to do."

Johnny tore his gaze from his sister's lest she see

through him and guess that his relationship with Shannon had crossed a line.

"No one's denying she's a strong woman," he said, "but Shannon's not stupid. Once her bone heals, she'll have weeks of physical therapy on her torn Achilles tendon. She'll have to concede victory to Rodriguez." Johnny didn't know who he hoped to convince—himself, his sister or the unconscious patient.

"My money is on Shannon that she'll recover and compete in Tucson." Dixie checked her watch. "Go on back to the ranch. I'll stay with her tonight."

He didn't want to let Shannon out of his sight—not with the vision of Heat Miser bearing down on her burned onto his brain. "Don't you have to open the gift shop in the morning?"

"Yes. I'll chug coffee all day to keep awake."

"That can't be good for your body if you're trying to make a baby."

"One time won't hurt."

"Listen, I don't mind sleeping in the chair tonight. I can catch a nap tomorrow."

"She's my best friend, Johnny."

I know. Dixie had always looked up to him with hero worship in her eyes but she'd be disappointed in him if she knew he'd slept with her best friend on a whim.

He played the guilt card. "Shannon will be mad at you if you neglect your health when you're trying to start a family."

Dixie stared at Shannon and nibbled her lower lip. "You promise you won't leave before I get here in the morning? I'll stop by on my way to the shop."

"I promise as long as you bring me a coffee and a doughnut."

"Done." She hugged him.

"Everything okay between you and Gavin?"

"Sure." She dropped her gaze. "Why?"

"You haven't called in a couple of days." She usually checked in with him every day.

"Gavin's had a rough week sleeping."

"Is he seeing his therapist?"

"Yes, but trying to get me pregnant is stressing him out."

"Maybe you should quit trying and let it happen when it happens."

"I suggested that but you know Gavin, once a soldier always a soldier. He's not surrendering until the plus sign appears on the home pregnancy test." She nodded to the bed. "If she wakes up, tell her I'll be by in the morning."

"Sure."

As soon as the door shut behind his sister, Johnny pulled the chair next to the bed and grasped Shannon's hand. He swore her fingers tightened against his. Satisfied that she knew she wasn't alone, he closed his eyes and tried to catch a few winks.

"THAT SMELL IS making me nauseous." Shannon scowled at her friends, who devoured greasy hamburgers at the foot of the hospital bed Monday afternoon. She'd awoken Sunday morning with a severe headache, which had only slightly dissipated over the past twenty-four hours, leaving her stomach feeling too queasy to eat.

Almost forty-eight hours had passed since her collision with Heat Miser, and despite being pumped full of pain medication she was uncomfortable and grumpy.

Skylar Riggins, a records transcriptionist for the Yuma Medical Center stuffed the remainder of her Big

Mac into her mouth. "When do you think you'll be able to go home?" she asked after swallowing her mouthful of burger.

"Wednesday," Shannon said.

Wendy Chin, a petite Asian woman who worked as a livestock insurance agent protested. "Isn't that too soon?"

"Not soon enough as far as I'm concerned." This morning they'd taken Shannon off the morphine pump and switched her to pills. So far she hadn't felt a difference in her pain level, which remained at a constant five on a scale of ten. Pain aside, she was eager to begin her rehab. Today was September second and every day counted if she intended to win the title of Cowgirl of the Year.

"If I had to guess, your father's not too happy with you right now." Julie Kenner knew all about dealing with unsupportive parents. Her mother hadn't spoken to her for a month after Julie had broken her arm in a Five Star Rodeo the previous summer.

"You'd guess right." Shannon's father had expressed his displeasure when he'd visited her late Sunday afternoon. He hadn't shown up yet today and she secretly hoped he'd find work at the ranch to detain him, because she wasn't in the mood for another lecture on how lucky she was to be alive. Then again, at least her father cared about her. Through the years she'd hardly ever thought of her estranged mother, but she'd woken this morning, wondering if the woman would even care that her daughter had survived a close call with a bull.

"Who gave you the teddy bear?" Skylar asked.

"One of my brothers." She doubted her father would waste money on a stuffed animal. The nurse had told her that her brothers had been by to see her Sunday night but she'd slept through their visit.

"Look on the bright side," said Kim Beaderman, a second-grade teacher in the Yuma school district, "now that your bull riding days are over, you'll grow closer to your father."

"Who said anything about quitting rodeo?" She wasn't washed up yet. She had a lot of rides left in her. If she walked away now, all she'd ever be was a cowgirl who had once ridden bulls.

"Whoa, girlfriend." Julie inched to the top of the bed and gently tapped Shannon's forehead. "Another collision with a bull's horns will leave you with more problems than memory loss when you're older." Julie believed she was an expert on human anatomy because she was an MRI technician.

No one knew her own body better than Shannon and she wasn't ready to hang up her bull rope. "Do any of you know if my score was higher than C.J.'s on Saturday?" She hadn't dared ask her father for fear that would start an argument. She'd been tempted to text Johnny but worried he'd also lecture her on quitting.

"You got an eighty-seven," Wendy said.

"No kidding?" An eighty-seven was her highest score to date. "Good. We're back to even."

Her cell phone rang and Shannon checked the caller I.D.—Dale Carson, a promoter for Dynasty Boots. "I have to take this call." Dale had left a voice message for her Sunday, asking her to contact him. Shannon had chickened out, figuring he wouldn't be pleased when he heard the extent of her injuries.

"We should get going." Wendy gathered the fast-food wrappers and dropped them into the trash can.

"Thanks for stopping by," Shannon said. Left alone in the room, she dialed Dale's number. He picked up on the first ring.

"Shannon?"

"It's me."

"Listen. I don't have a lot of time right now, but the PR team has come up with a new idea."

She rolled her eyes. She hadn't been a fan of the "pretend romance" plot and doubted she'd like their new idea any better. "What is it?"

"First, how are you feeling?"

At least he'd asked. "Better, thanks."

"I spoke with your doctor yesterday."

So much for doctor-patient confidentiality.

"He believes the earliest you can ride again is six-to-eight weeks. That puts us in the middle of October or early November, which means we stand to lose a lot of money in ticket sales."

"I'll work hard at my rehab and be back in four weeks." She'd say and do anything to save her chances of winning a national title.

"Take the eight weeks. We've got a new game plan."

She braced herself.

"After that scene involving you, C.J. and Johnny Cash behind the chutes this past Saturday we've had hundreds of fan emails, letters and phone calls asking about the Man in Black."

"What about Johnny?"

"What's going on between you two?"

"He's my best friend's brother. We've known each other for years."

"So you're just friends?"

"Yes."

"Dynasty Boots wants to promote a love-triangle between you, Johnny Cash and C.J. The fans are going to soak it up."

Good God. "You want Johnny and C.J. to fight over me?"

"That's right. We're working on booking appearances at a couple of rodeo venues, so fans can see the three of you together."

"And if Johnny refuses to be part of this charade?"

"Talk him into it, Shannon, because you won't like the alternative."

The alternative being that Dynasty Boots would cancel their contract with her.

Chapter Five

"What are you doing here?"

"I see you're ready to bust out of this joint." Johnny removed his Stetson and stepped into Shannon's hospital room late Wednesday afternoon.

She lay on the bed with her broken leg propped up on a pillow. After she'd eaten lunch and her nurse had helped her shower, the doctor had signed her release papers. She caught herself fussing with her still damp hair and silently cursed. Why did she care what Johnny thought of her looks?

Maybe because you slept with him.

Johnny approached the bed and the familiar scent of sandalwood and musk reminded Shannon of pressing her nose against his neck, his naked chest, his... She clutched her teddy bear, as if the stuffed animal would protect her from the memories.

"I thought my father was picking me up?"

"He was on his way, but the truck blew a tire and he didn't have a spare. He's waiting for a tow outside Stagecoach."

"So you're stuck giving me a ride."

"It's no trouble."

"If it was, you wouldn't say so."

"Be nice." His lips twitched and the tension she'd felt when he first entered the room dissipated.

"Sorry. I've still got a nagging headache." Unconsciously she stroked her hand over the head of her bed buddy.

"Did you name your new friend?" He nodded to the teddy bear.

"Not yet." She set the stuffed animal aside. "I don't even know who bought it."

"I did."

Her heart thumped a little harder. "I don't recall you visiting."

"I stayed with you Saturday night then left Sunday morning when Dixie got here."

"My dad didn't make you—"

"No. I—" he cleared his throat "—wanted to stay."

His admission resurrected the strain between them, leaving Shannon speechless.

"Dixie had a favorite monkey she used to sleep with," he said.

"Cocoa. Remember the day his arm fell off?"

He chuckled. "I thought Dixie had been mortally wounded when I heard her scream echo through the orchard."

"Then you sewed Cocoa's arm back on. You're a good big brother, Johnny." She made eye contact with him, but he looked away before she could guess if what he felt for her was brotherly affection or something more.

Enough talk about brotherly-sisterly love. "What happened after Heat Miser head butted me? I heard the buzzer but everything after that is a blank."

His shoulders stiffened.

"C'mon, Johnny. You were there. You saw the whole thing."

His chest shuddered with a long exhale and he closed his eyes. "Heat Miser freight-trained you."

She flinched.

"After you fell off, the bullfighters distracted Heat Miser for a second before he turned on you."

"Was I trying to get to my feet?" she asked.

"You weren't moving at all."

She swallowed hard as she envisioned herself lying motionless on the arena floor. "Then what happened?"

It must have been a trick of the fluorescent ceiling light because it looked as if Johnny's eyes glistened with moisture. "Heat Miser charged, lowered his head and flung you into the air."

Suddenly taking a deep breath became impossible as an invisible weight settled on Shannon's chest. It was a miracle she hadn't broken her neck or suffered internal injuries. Fearing her anxiety would escalate if she focused on her close call with death, she said, "I wish I'd seen the look on C.J.'s face after I evened the score between us."

"You went out with a bang that's for sure."

"What do you mean 'went out'?"

"You're finished with rodeo." He frowned. "Aren't you?"

That Johnny assumed she'd quit the sport after her bad wreck stung. It was bad enough that her father and brothers believed she should retire—easy for them to say when they'd won a title. "A broken leg doesn't mean I'm washed up." Shoot, her bone would heal in six weeks. By the time January arrived, she'd be ready for the rodeo in Tucson. Not wanting to argue about her rodeo career she changed the subject. "How do you like your new job as foreman?"

"Your dad's a fair man. I have no complaints."

"Has he heard from Uncle Roger?"

"Roger made it to Florida. He traded his saddle in for a fishing pole and spends his mornings at the pier, entertaining fishermen with ranching stories."

"I'm glad he's happy."

"The only one who's not happy with how things worked out is Hank."

"Poor baby. He misses Roger."

"I have to tie him up when I leave or he'll run away."

"I'll take him off your hands. It'll be nice to have company in the house while I'm recuperating."

He grabbed the plastic hospital bags stuffed with her clothes. "Is this all you have?"

She nodded.

"I'll let the nurses know you're ready to leave."

Shannon stared at the empty doorway. Were they going to talk about the night they spent together at the Hacienda Motel or continue to pretend it never happened?

JOHNNY WAS INSTRUCTED to bring his truck to the front entrance and wait for Shannon there. He wasn't looking forward to the drive to the ranch. They couldn't keep pretending they hadn't slept together. If the sex hadn't blown his mind, he'd have set things straight between them, but knowing how good Shannon had felt in his arms made everything more complicated.

When he reached his truck, he flipped on the air to cool the interior and drove to the front entrance where Shannon waited in a wheelchair. He placed her crutches across the floor behind the front seats, then reached for her.

"I don't need help," she said.

Ignoring her, he lifted her from the chair, holding her close for a few seconds before depositing her in the passenger seat and securing her belt. After he shut the door, he tipped his hat to the nurse. "Have a nice day, ma'am."

"We can stop for a bite to eat if you're hungry," he said when he got behind the wheel.

"I'm not hungry."

He left the parking lot and merged with traffic before glancing across the seat. Shannon's eyes were closed, lips pressed tightly together. "You okay?"

"I feel like I'm going to throw up."

He turned down a side street and put the truck in Park, then dumped her belongings onto the backseat and handed her the empty plastic bag. "Just in case."

"Thanks."

"Would you be more comfortable in the backseat with your leg up?"

"No. I just want to get home."

He put in a George Strait CD, hoping the music would take her mind off her queasy stomach, and drove through downtown Yuma.

"Johnny?"

"What?"

"We need to talk."

Oh, hell. Here it comes.

The truck hit a pothole in the road and Shannon grimaced in pain when her leg bumped the door. "Relax," he said. "There's plenty of time to talk later."

Once he hit the open road, he put the pedal to the metal. When they arrived at the outskirts of Stagecoach, he noticed Clive's truck was missing from the side of the road. "Looks like your dad got his tire fixed." He peeked at Shannon. Beads of perspiration dotted her brow. "When can you take another pain pill?"

"Not for two hours."

Fifteen minutes later he pulled into the ranch yard. "Sit tight." He glanced toward the barn on his way to open the passenger-side door. Clive's truck was nowhere in sight. "I'll carry you inside," he said. Because she was in a lot of pain *not* because the few seconds he'd held her outside the hospital hadn't been nearly enough.

She didn't protest when he lifted her into his arms. Although small in stature, she was solid muscle, except for the soft curve of her breast, which pressed against his chest as he strode toward the house. He paused in the foyer. "Where to?" In all the years he'd worked part-time for Clive, he'd never set foot inside the house.

"Upstairs. The bedroom at the end of the hall."

Shannon's room was exactly as he'd envisioned—plain. Beige walls. Beige bedding. Even the wingback chair by the window was beige. He laid her on the bed. "Is there an extra pillow for your leg?"

"Linen closet in the hallway."

Once Shannon was situated, Johnny fetched her personal belongings and crutches from the truck. Back in her bedroom he plugged in her cell phone charger, then moved the nightstand closer to the bed.

"Johnny?"

"What?"

"Did you get my gear from the arena?"

"Rodriguez dropped off your bag and laptop at the hospital after the rodeo. Your dad brought them back to the ranch."

"I can't believe I forgot to ask about my gear until now," she said.

"You've been high on pain meds for the past four days." Johnny removed the plastic bottle of pills from his pocket and set it on the nightstand. "I'll get you a drink."

"There should be bottles of water in the fridge."

A few minutes later, he returned with two bottles of water, a box of saltines and her laptop. "Your computer was sitting on the kitchen table."

"Thanks."

"Anything else I can get you before I head to the barn?" Their gazes clashed and the bold way she stared at him sent up a warning flag inside his head.

"There's something I need to ask you," she said.

He thought he'd be ready for this conversation, but he wasn't. Not after carrying Shannon inside and feeling her body nestled against his. He snapped his fingers. "Let me fetch you an extra blanket." He found one in the linen closet, then sagged against the wall. Was she going to tell him their night in the motel had been a mistake? He hoped so and he hoped not.

When he went back into the bedroom, she was sound asleep. Her skin was the color of bleached flour, its paleness accentuated by the tangled strands of her jet-black hair. Her vulnerability struck him hard.

He didn't understand her obsession with riding bulls. The only thing he knew for sure was that he hated seeing her suffer. He wanted to believe the need to keep her safe was rooted in his big-brother feelings toward her, but it wasn't. The days of viewing Shannon as his little sister's best friend were long gone. Now, when he looked at her, he saw a sexy, mature woman he was attracted to. A woman he wanted.

A woman you need to keep the hell away from.

There was too much riding on his job at the Triple D to mess things up by becoming involved with the boss's daughter. He closed the blinds, blocking out the afternoon sun. Worried she'd wake up chilled he covered her with the extra blanket then left.

He went to the barn and finished mucking the stall he'd been working on when Clive had asked him to pick up Shannon from the hospital. Afterward, he went to the foreman's cabin and unchained Hank, then escorted him inside to the bathroom. When he ran the water in the tub, Hank whirled and bumped his snout against the closed door. "I know. Baths suck, but if you want to be invited into a woman's bed, you can't stink." Johnny set Hank in the tub and drizzled shampoo along his back.

Hank sneezed.

"Get ready, boy. This stuff is supposed to—" he read the label "—unlock dangerous levels of attraction."

Hank didn't buy the claim. He shook from head to toe, spraying the bathroom walls with suds.

A short while later, Johnny towel-dried the dog and opened the door. Hank made a mad dash into the main room where he rolled himself dry on the rug. Johnny gathered the wet towels. When he left the bathroom, he jumped inside his skin.

"Crap, Dixie." He slapped a hand over his pounding heart. "You can't just walk in here without knocking."

"I did knock." She petted Hank while Johnny went into the laundry off the kitchen and stuffed the wet towels into the machine. "What are you doing here?"

"I brought a few dinners over for you and Shannon." Had Shannon told his sister what they'd done and now Dixie assumed they were a couple? "Why would you think Shannon and I eat together?"

"Hey, don't get testy. I wanted to bring you a house-warming gift, so I made your favorite casseroles." She pointed to the cardboard box on the kitchen table, "Since I was going to all that trouble, I made extra for Shannon, because Clive doesn't cook much."

"That was nice of you, Dix." He peered into the box at the ceramic dishes covered in foil. "Shannon's sleeping right now. I'll take them up to the house later."

Dixie placed the dishes in the fridge then hugged him.

"What's that for?"

"Because you're such a nice guy."

And nice guys finish last.

"I wish I could stay and visit but I need to make a run into town for Hank's dog food." The mutt's ears perked at the mention of his name.

"Doesn't Clive pay for his food?"

Johnny didn't know and he hadn't asked and frankly he didn't care. He was feeling hemmed in and looking for an excuse to leave the ranch. Clive had hired him to take care of the horses and cattle, not babysit his daughter and a geriatric dog. He pulled his truck keys from his pocket and Dixie preceded him outside.

"Thanks again for bringing the food." He waited for his sister to drive off before he headed to the main highway. As the mile markers passed, he convinced himself that he'd better devise a game plan for dealing with what had happened between him and Shannon. If he didn't, the awkwardness between them would grow, and then Clive would notice and ask questions Johnny didn't care to answer.

When he pulled into Baine Feed and Tack, he noticed

Clive's pickup, sporting a new rear tire, was parked in the lot. He opened the glove compartment to put his sunglasses away and an envelope dropped onto the floor. The letter from the IRS had arrived a week ago, informing Johnny that he owed five thousand dollars in back taxes on the farm, because of an exemption he'd claimed but hadn't been entitled to. He should have paid a professional to do the taxes, but he'd hoped to save money. He hadn't figured out how he'd pay the penalty and worried what his siblings would say when they found out their big brother had screwed up.

He placed the envelope back in the compartment and entered the feed store. Clive and Jim were nowhere in sight, but he heard voices echoing from the storeroom. Johnny wandered over to the pet food aisle and found the brand Roger fed Hank, and then he browsed the dog toys. The sound of boot heels clunking against the floor warned him he had company.

"You've got my sympathy, Clive," Jim said. "I don't know what I'd do if one of my daughter's fell off the deep end and engaged in extreme activities."

Fell off the deep end?

"At least I won't have to worry about her breaking her neck anymore. After this last accident, she's finished with rodeo," Clive said.

Evidently Shannon hadn't told her father she had no plans to quit the sport.

"You want me to send Maryellen by to check in on Shannon tomorrow?" Jim asked.

"That's nice of you to offer, Jim, but my daughter's stubborn to the core. She won't take help from anyone."

"Wonder who she inherited that trait from?" Jim laughed.

Johnny took the dog food and a large rawhide bone up to the checkout.

Jim noticed him first. "Didn't know you were in the store, Johnny."

"Thought I'd buy Roger's hound a present." He nodded to his boss. "Clive."

"That'll be thirty-seven eighty-three," Jim said.

Johnny set two twenties on the counter. After Jim handed him the change, he said, "See you next time."

"Wait up."

Clive followed Johnny out of the store. "I've got a favor to ask of you."

Johnny set the bag of dog food in the truck. "What kind of favor?"

"While I was waiting for the tow truck this afternoon, Jeb Russell phoned and he wants me to deliver the cutting horses he bought a week early. I'm leaving for Wyoming in the morning."

"But—"

"I know the timing is bad with Shannon just getting out of the hospital." Clive frowned. "But after Kendall backed out of buying Pepper a month ago, money is tight. I need this sale."

Johnny knew all about tight budgets.

"I'd appreciate you looking after Shannon until I get back."

"How long do you plan to be gone?"

"About a week. I want to swing by the Bar Seven outside Durango and see if I can't talk Bill Cunningham into buying a new stud for his mares." He twirled his hat in his hand. "I realize checking in on my daughter isn't the job you signed on for, but Matt and Luke are wrapped up in that murder trial and they don't have time to drive out to the ranch."

"I'll keep an eye on her." Nothing like throwing temptation in his face every day.

"I appreciate that, Johnny."

A week alone at the ranch with Shannon and no chaperone—God help him. They needed to have that *talk* ASAP.

SHANNON STOOD AT her bedroom window, leaning on her crutches. She'd awoken from her nap to a desperate need to use the bathroom and had managed to shuffle across the hall without help. She'd suffered rodeo injuries before, but this was the first time she'd broken a bone and the pain and discomfort were more than she'd bargained for.

The dull throb pulsing through her mending tibia demanded she climb back in bed and prop her leg up on the pillow, until she saw Johnny's truck barreling up the road with her father following behind him.

Johnny parked at the foreman's cabin and went inside while her father stopped in front of the house. A minute later the front door opened and footsteps clomped up the stairs. Her father appeared in the doorway.

"Hey, Dad."

"What are you doing out of bed?"

"I had to use the bathroom."

He glanced away. Discussing bodily functions, especially the female kind, embarrassed him. She remembered the horrified look on his face the day he'd caught her peeing against the barn. When he'd asked her what she was doing, her explanation had almost given him a heart attack. She'd insisted she wanted to pee on things just like her brothers did. As a kid, her only role models had been her brothers and the one thing she'd yet to do that they'd accomplished was win a national rodeo title.

Shannon staggered to the bed and sat down. Using both hands she lifted her injured leg onto the stack of pillows and leaned against the headboard.

"I meant to pick you up from the hospital, but—"

"Johnny told me the truck blew a tire." Why was it so hard for her father to show his affection?

"How long did the doc say it would be until your leg heals?"

"He'll x-ray the bone in six weeks and if everything looks good, I'll begin physical therapy then."

"There's no need to rush your recovery."

If her father expected her to sit on her butt and allow her muscles to weaken, he was in for a big surprise. "I won't do anything to risk injuring my leg before the bone is healed."

"Don't forget your head."

She smiled. "No worries. Last time I checked it was still attached to my body."

Her humor didn't go over well and he scowled. "It's not funny, Shannon. If you fall and smack your noggin you could—"

"I'll be careful."

"I'm leaving in the morning to take a horse up to Wyoming. Won't be back for a week."

"I'll be fine." Good grief, she wasn't bedridden.

"You'll let Johnny know if you need help or—" he nodded to the bottle of pills on the nightstand "—your medication refilled at the pharmacy."

"I will."

"Call me if you need anything."

It was nice of him to offer, but she was positive he hoped she wouldn't contact him. "Be careful driving." Then he was gone.

Tears stung her eyes as she stared at the ceiling. A droplet of moisture rolled down her cheek and she wiped it away. Crying was for babies and she wasn't a baby.

She was a bull rider.

Chapter Six

"Look who came for a visit," Buck said, glancing up from the playing cards in his hand.

"It's Saturday night. I expected everyone to be at a rodeo or a bar." Johnny shut the door and joined Buck and Will at the picnic-sized table the brothers had built for the bunkhouse.

Only three days had passed since Johnny had brought Shannon home from the hospital, but with Clive out of town being all alone with her at the ranch was driving him nuts. Twice today she'd texted that she needed to talk with him, but he'd made excuses and put her off. He knew they needed to confront what they'd done in Gila Bend, but for reasons he didn't understand, he kept chickening out.

"Porter and Conway drove over to Tubac for the Old World Rodeo Days," Will said. "Conway made it to the final round, so they won't be home until tomorrow."

"You want in?" Buck nodded to the deck of cards.

"No, thanks."

Buck dropped a piece of candy into the pot. "I'll raise you one Smartie."

"I stopped by to check on the place," Johnny said.

Will added a piece of candy to the pot. "Did you think we'd destroy the bunkhouse once you moved out?"

There were no broken furniture, dents in the walls or stains on the cement floor. His brothers must be taking their squabbles outside. "Any leaks?" Two nights ago a storm had passed through the area, dumping a half inch of rain in less than an hour.

"The place is airtight," Will said.

Will had a background in construction and had drawn up the plans for the bunkhouse, and then all the brothers had helped rough-in the plumbing and electrical before pouring the cement slab and installing the metal sides and roof. His siblings had protested trading in their full-size beds for twin beds, but in doing so, they'd left space for the picnic table, refrigerator and sink at one end of the room and a small bathroom, two sofas and two chairs that sat at the other end. In the middle was a row of single beds facing the opposite wall where a large flat-screen TV hung.

"What's up with all the rodeo posters?" Johnny asked.

"Porter watches that design show *Dear Genevieve*. He's got a big ol' crush on that woman." Buck rolled his eyes. "According to Genevieve, wallpaper gives any place a homey feel."

"Porter wanted to put up some fleur-de-lis French crap," Will said. "But we vetoed that and voted for the posters."

"The photos of raging bulls and ominous buck-ing stock warm this place right up." Johnny grinned. "Where's Mack's band playing tonight?"

"They're not. Mack pulled the weekend shift at the dude ranch," Buck said.

Caught up in his responsibilities at the Triple D Johnny

had forgotten Mack had recently hired on as a wrangler at the Blackjack Mountain Dude Ranch. "How does he like the job?"

"He hasn't said much about it." Buck laid down his cards. "Four of a kind."

"You lose." Will showed a full house, then swept the pile of candy to his side of the table. "How's Shannon?"

"She's fine." Not wanting to field questions about his boss's daughter, Johnny scooted his chair back and stood. "Is Dixie inside? I didn't see her truck parked in the yard."

"She's here. Her truck's at Troy's garage," Buck said.

"What happened to it?" Johnny asked.

Buck shuffled the deck. "Stalled outside Yuma yesterday."

"Why didn't she call me?"

Will snorted. "You forgetting she's married? Gavin picked her up and made arrangements for a tow."

Johnny ignored the sharp twinge he felt at being knocked off the pedestal his sister had put him on all those years. "What's wrong with the truck?"

"Alternator went out," Buck said. "Troy had to order a new one."

Buck had worked for the local mechanic on and off for the past five years and Johnny thought his brother should ask Troy if he could buy into his business and become a partner. Buck was a natural at fixing engines.

"How's the construction business?" Johnny asked Will. His brother worked for a small family-run construction company owned and operated by Ben Wallace, a former high-school classmate of Will's.

"Things are slow right now," Will said.

"I better say hello to Dixie before I take off."

Buck's voice stopped Johnny at the door. "Come back anytime you get homesick." His brothers chuckled.

On the way to the farmhouse Johnny paused to stare at the setting sun and recalled the afternoons he'd walked with his grandfather through the groves, listening to the old man talk about the life cycle of the pecan.

You're the eldest, Johnny. I'm counting on you to keep these trees in the family.

Johnny hadn't cared about the nuts, but he'd worshipped his grandfather and had made a solemn promise to fulfill his wishes. He walked to the front of the house, then entered without knocking as he'd done his whole life. He took one step toward the kitchen and froze. A feminine moaning sound drifted into the hallway.

Face burning hotter than a pancake skillet, Johnny did an about-face and made a dash for the door, but the tip of his boot clipped his grandmother's umbrella stand and sent it crashing to the floor.

"Johnny?" His sister stood in the kitchen doorway, wearing only a bathrobe, her hair mussed and her lips swollen. "What's wrong?"

Flustered, he said, "Don't you think you ought to lock the door if you and Gavin plan to carry on like that in the house?"

Her eyes widened. "We weren't *doing it* in the kitchen. I was making Gavin an ice cream float."

Irritated that she mocked him, he scowled, which only egged her on more.

"I always make Gavin a float after we…you know… as a reward for being ready and willing anytime."

Ready and willing? "What the heck are you talking about?"

"My temperature, stupid."

"What does your temperature have to do with having sex?"

"I'm ovulating, so we're—"

"I get it." Johnny's anger died a quick death and he felt like an idiot for badgering her. "Sorry, I stopped by to ask you for a favor, but we can talk later."

"Stay."

Johnny trailed Dixie into the kitchen where she stopped at Gavin's side and kissed his cheek.

Of all his siblings, Johnny was closest to Dixie and he missed not being the apple of his baby sister's eye. Gavin nodded to Johnny but neither man made eye contact.

As Dixie helped Gavin make the floats, she asked, "What's this favor you need?"

"I was hoping you could stop by the Triple D tomorrow and spend time with Shannon while I repair a section of fence along the highway."

"Are you asking me to babysit her?" Dixie smiled.

"Clive's out of town and he put me in charge of keeping tabs on Shannon so I've been sticking close to the ranch house." Johnny crossed his arms over his chest. "I've got to fix the break in the fence before I move the cattle into that area next week."

"I could open the shop for you tomorrow," Gavin said.

"You sure?"

Gavin nodded.

Dixie texted on her cell phone. "I told Shannon that I'd be over around eight in the morning."

"Thanks, Dixie." Johnny knew his sister would come through for him.

"How do you like having the foreman's cabin all to yourself?" Gavin asked.

"The quiet takes getting used to." He steered the conversation to Gavin's work on a water reclamation project for the city of Yuma and a half hour passed before Johnny stood. "I better go." He shook hands with Gavin.

"I'll walk you outside," Dixie said. When they stopped at his truck she spoke. "I'm worried about Shannon."

"Why? What did she say in her text?"

"Nothing, but we talked on the phone yesterday and she sounded depressed."

"You can cheer her up when you see her tomorrow." He hopped into the truck.

"Why don't you stop in town and buy her a bouquet of flowers? That will brighten her room."

I don't think so. Until he and Shannon figured out what that night in Gila Bend was all about, he didn't dare do anything that would give Shannon the wrong impression about his feelings—whatever the hell they were—for her.

"Shannon's always looked up to you as a big brother."

Why was he everyone's big brother?

"Back in tenth grade she said I was the luckiest girl in the world because I had you for a big brother and she wished Matt and Luke treated her as nice."

"I've known her brothers for years. They're not mean."

"No, but they never make time for Shannon." Dixie leaned into the truck and kissed his cheek. "Watch over her, okay?"

Johnny shut the door and started the engine. He doubted Dixie would have asked him to look out for her best friend if she'd known he'd already slept with her.

"Ouch." Shannon winced when Dixie pulled too hard on her hair.

Dixie smiled at Shannon in the mirror. "Bull riders aren't supposed to whine."

Shannon sighed. "Thanks for helping me."

"You hate that, don't you?"

"Hate what?"

"Needing help," Dixie said.

"I was raised to be independent. If I'd had a grandmother who cared about me the way yours cared about you, I might not be stubborn."

Dixie separated Shannon's hair into three plaits and braided the ebony strands. "Do you know that my grandma wanted to adopt you?"

"No way."

"Yes way. Grandma Ada would get so angry when you showed up at the farm with dirty hair and wax in your ears."

Shannon shuddered. "Remember the afternoon I got my period?"

Both women laughed.

"And your grandfather's stunned face when we burst into the kitchen and blurted that I was dying of some terrible disease because I had blood in my underwear."

Dixie laughed so hard tears escaped her eyes. "Grandpa fled the house as if his overalls were on fire."

"Then your grandma came inside and took us both upstairs to the bathroom and explained how a woman's body worked and how to use the supplies she'd been keeping on hand for you when your time came," Shannon said.

"Grandma Ada loved you as much as she loved me, Shannon."

"I kept the quilt she made for me."

"She'd be happy about that." Dixie wrapped the end of the braid in an elastic band. "You know, every time we've talked about family it's always been mine."

"Your family is more entertaining."

"I'm serious." Dixie set the comb on the nightstand, then lifted Shannon's broken leg onto the bed and arranged the pillows beneath it. "You never mention your mother."

"Why would I? She walked out on my dad when I was a toddler and I haven't had any contact with her since."

"She's never called you through the years?"

"Never. I overheard Matt and Luke talking about her once and I asked why she never visited us." Shannon swallowed hard. After all these years it remained difficult to accept that her mother wanted nothing to do with her or her brothers. "Matt said she'd married an older man who didn't have kids and moved out of state with him."

"Where did she meet the guy?"

"I don't know and if my dad knows he'd never say."

"That's rough. I'm sorry."

Shannon blew off the sympathy. "I'm not the only kid on the block who grew up with a parent who didn't care about them. Your father didn't want anything to do with you or Johnny."

"I might not have cared if our mother had paid more attention to us kids instead of spending her time searching for the perfect man."

It was common knowledge that Aimee Cash's boys had all been fathered by different men—none of whom she'd married. Most folks claimed Aimee had died of a broken heart, but there had been rumors that she'd overdosed on antidepressant pills.

"At least we had our grandparents. They loved us," Dixie said.

"Wouldn't it be nice if every kid had a childhood

where both parents loved them?" Shannon said. "Speaking of childhoods…any news on the baby front?"

"Not yet, but the trying is fun."

After their laughter died down, Shannon struggled to find a way to bring up the subject of Johnny. The longer he avoided her, the more doubts trickled into her mind. Before she considered how it would sound, she blurted, "I heard Johnny and Charlene broke up."

If the change in subject startled Dixie, she didn't show it. "Johnny said they'd been growing apart for a while." She shook her head. "How does that happen to people? They stay together all those years and then call it quits without a backward glance."

"I don't know." Shannon had never been in a long-term relationship.

"After all Gavin and I went through, if he left me, I'd never survive the heartache."

"It's too bad about Johnny and Charlene," Shannon said, not feeling a bit sorry for the other woman.

"Speaking of relationships," Dixie said. "I'm worried you're still nursing a broken heart over C.J."

"Why would you think that?"

"When we talked on the phone the other day, you sounded down in the dumps."

"I'm over C.J. He can have all the buckle bunnies he wants and I don't care."

"I never could figure out what you saw in him," Dixie said.

"There's a lot more to C.J. than the public sees."

"Like what?"

"He wouldn't want me to share it with anyone, Dixie." She'd promised C.J. she'd never tell anyone about his dysfunctional family. "Like us, he didn't have a great childhood, either." The problem with C.J. was that he didn't trust anyone's feelings for him and therefore couldn't remain in a committed relationship.

"How are you and your dad getting along?" Dixie asked.

"Fine, why?"

"C'mon, Shannon, this is me you're talking to." Dixie rummaged through the cosmetic bag she'd brought to the house and held up two bottles of polish. "Vampire Red or Sorority Pink?"

"I don't need my nails done," Shannon protested.

"I went to all the work of giving you a pedicure—"

"Which I didn't ask for, but thank you anyway."

"Amuse me and let me paint your toenails."

"Fine. Go ahead."

"Which color?" Dixie asked.

"I don't care."

"You're more vampire than sorority girl. We'll go with red."

Shannon snorted. "Since when did you get into all this foolishness?"

"I own a gift shop that sells natural beauty products. I have to walk the talk if I want to convince customers that my soaps will make their skin look smooth and beautiful." Dixie placed a foam form between Shannon's toes, then applied a base coat on the nails. "Besides, men like painted toenails."

"Men don't notice a woman's feet."

"Oh, yes, they do." Dixie's eyes twinkled. "Until I met Gavin, I never knew that toes could play a role in foreplay."

"Stop. I don't want to hear any more." Shannon covered her ears.

Dixie applied the first coat of red polish and Shannon admired her toes—they didn't look half-bad.

"What are Matt and Luke up to these days?" Dixie asked.

"Busy preparing for a trial."

"What kind of case are they working on?"

"They're prosecuting a man for a gang-related murder along the border. Matt phoned the other day, but we didn't talk long before he got another call."

Dixie put away the polish and admired her handiwork. "You're all set." She straightened the blanket on the bed. "Next time I visit, I'll give you a manicure."

"Dixie…"

"What?"

"Thank you."

"Text me if you need anything." Dixie hugged Shannon.

As soon as the downstairs door shut, a feeling of melancholy swept through Shannon. At times she was jealous of Dixie and the love she and Gavin shared.

"Stop being a brat." She had nothing to be sad about. She was making a name for herself in bull riding, and pretty soon she'd win a national title, which would prove she was the best rodeo cowgirl in the country.

A BANGING ON the door roused Johnny at midnight. Hank barked from his pillow on the kitchen floor and he shushed the dog as he thrust his legs into the jeans he'd left on the floor by the bed. He wondered which one of his brothers had stopped by for a late-night visit.

"Shannon," he said when he opened the door.

She moved past him on her crutches and entered the cabin. "I know it's late but—" Her crutch caught on the edge of the rug and if not for his quick reflexes as he grabbed her around the waist, she'd have landed on her face. "Whoa." He steadied her, his fingers enjoying the feel of her trim tummy. Reluctantly he released her and retrieved the fallen crutch. He noticed her perspiring face. "You shouldn't have walked all the way over here."

"I wouldn't have to go anywhere on my crutches if you'd stop avoiding me."

"I'm not avoiding you." Embarrassed, he went to the fridge and got a bottle of water, then nodded to the sofa.

"We need to talk, Johnny."

She was right. He'd been running away from this discussion for three weeks. "Okay." When he handed her the water he noticed the toenails peeking out of the cast on her leg were painted red.

She caught him looking and said, "Your sister gave me a pedicure this morning." She patted the cushion next to her, but he chose to sit in the chair. He'd gotten a whiff of bath soap and clean woman when she'd stumbled into his arms and there was no way he could sit next to her and not be tempted to touch her.

"About that night—" he said.

"My rodeo promoter Dale Carson's been calling me nonstop."

Startled, Johnny asked, "He's not pushing you to come back before you're ready, is he?"

"No. But there's been a development since the Yuma rodeo."

"What kind of development?"

"Apparently the rodeo fans that afternoon enjoyed the show you and C.J. put on behind the chutes."

"What show?"

"Your scuffle?"

Johnny's face reddened.

"The fans think you, me and C.J. are involved in some sort of love triangle."

"What?"

"Dale said they've gotten hundreds of emails wanting to know who the Man In Black is."

He waved a hand. "It'll die down in another week or so."

"That's exactly what Dynasty Boots is afraid will happen if you and C.J. don't vie for my attention in public."

What? "They want us to come to blows over you?"

"I don't believe they expect you to take it that far, but they want to keep fans interested in my competition with C.J., so they don't lose ticket sales while my leg is healing."

"No." He bolted from the chair and paced across the floor.

"Dale said he'd make it worth your while."

"What do you mean?"

"If you're willing to show up with me at two of C.J.'s upcoming events, Dynasty Boots will pay you five thousand dollars."

Five thousand dollars?

She smiled. "It's not bad for playacting."

Johnny was still contemplating the money angle and it took a moment for the rest of her words to sink in. *Playacting?* What they'd shared in the motel room in Gila Bend sure hadn't been playacting. Did she think it would be that easy to carry out this charade?

"Dale wants me and you to attend C.J.'s rodeo in Winslow at the end of September."

"You shouldn't be gallivanting all over the state with a broken leg."

"Whether you take the money from Dynasty Boots and help me out or not, I'm going to Winslow."

"You can't drive with a cast on your leg."

She reached for her crutches. "I use my right foot on the gas pedal and the brake."

Johnny beat her to the door. "Let me take you up to the house in the truck."

"No, thanks. I need the exercise."

He stepped outside with her and held the crutches as she hopped down the porch steps.

"This is crazy, Shannon."

"It's five grand, two rodeos and a little playacting." She took her crutches from him. "What are you afraid of?"

Plenty.

"Text me your answer tomorrow. I told Dale I'd get back to him by Monday night."

Johnny watched Shannon hobble up to the house. Once she'd made it inside, he shut the door. Five thousand dollars was a lot of money—money that would pay the tax bill sitting in his truck.

But playacting? How the hell would he pull that off when he'd already experienced the payoff after all those heated looks and teasing touches?

Chapter Seven

The last Saturday in September Johnny stood next to Clive, one boot propped on the bottom rail of the corral and watched a cutting horse named Odyssey trot in circles. "How's his temperament?" Johnny asked.

"Good. Doesn't need much direction when you're in the saddle."

"You plan to sell him?"

"Depends—" Clive lifted the empty feed bucket off the ground and clanged it against the rail. Startled, Odyssey reared, pawing the air. "—on whether or not I can cure his fear of loud noises."

"If you want me to work with him, let me know," Johnny said.

"You're doing me a favor by driving Shannon up to Winslow today."

Shannon hadn't told her father about the love-triangle idea Dynasty Boots had come up with to entertain rodeo fans, and Johnny wasn't about to spill the beans now.

Three weeks had passed since Shannon had talked him into accepting the boot company's offer of five thousand dollars and still neither one of them had brought up their one-night stand in Gila Bend.

"Don't know why Shannon's sponsor is making her

show up at a rodeo she can't compete in," Clive said, "but I suppose she's getting antsy. Can't recall the last time she stayed at the ranch for more than a few days."

Truth be told, Johnny was becoming antsy, too—not to leave the ranch but to settle things between him and Shannon. He'd done a heck of a job avoiding her since Clive had come back from Wyoming, but she was still on his mind morning until night.

"Watching the bull rides from the stands might give her a different perspective on the sport," Johnny said. Maybe she wouldn't be as eager to get back in the arena.

"I never should have allowed her to enter those mutton-bustin' contests with Luke and Matt."

"Doubt you could have stopped her. As long as I've known Shannon, she's been determined to keep up with her brothers."

"I thought she'd outgrow her tomboy ways, but she never did." Clive shook his head. "I suppose not having a mother didn't help."

"Shannon's made a name for herself in rodeo and she's brought a lot of awareness to women's bull riding."

"I'd rather my daughter makes a name for herself cooking or running a gift shop like Dixie. At least I wouldn't have to worry about her breaking her neck."

The front door of the house opened and Shannon stepped out. A week ago the doctor had put her in a walking boot, and she was moving around with ease now. "I guess we're ready to roll." He and Clive met Shannon at Johnny's truck, which he'd parked in front of the house.

"Dad, I'll text you when we leave Winslow late this afternoon." She flashed her father a smile.

"Take your time," Clive said.

Johnny felt bad for the pair—the father and daughter

loved each other, but they also disappointed each other. "We've got a five-hour drive ahead of us. We'd better get on the road if you need to be there by noon."

Johnny honked as he pulled away. Sixty minutes into the trip and he was sweating from the tension in the cab. "Need to stop?" he asked when he passed the sign for Riverdale.

"No."

Her sullenness irritated him. "What's the matter?"

She finally looked at him. "You really don't know?"

A sinking feeling settled in his gut. He gripped the wheel as if it was a life raft and guided the truck to the side of the road and shifted into Park.

"What are you doing?" she asked. "We'll be late for the rodeo."

"We might as well get this over with."

"Hey, if you'd rather forget that we slept together, just say so." She chopped the air with her hand. "Done."

Shannon was right—they'd be late for the rodeo if he didn't get back on the road. He shifted into Drive and merged into his lane. "You never brought it up until now, so I assumed you didn't want to discuss it."

She gasped. "You think I do one-night stands all the time?"

"No!" The skin over his knuckles glowed white and threatened to split open. "I just thought, you know…"

"No, I don't know, Johnny. I have no idea what that night means to you. Why don't you tell me?"

He gaped at her.

"Watch the road!"

Johnny straightened the wheel and the truck swerved back into the lane. "If you were expecting all kinds of flowery compliments and—"

"Do I look like the kind of woman who needs a man to praise her?" Then she added, "I just assumed you didn't want to talk about that night because you didn't enjoy it."

"Enjoy it?" Now he was mad. He wasn't a Don Juan by any means but he'd never had a woman not know he didn't enjoy making love to her. The stress from days of ignoring his attraction to Shannon, days of agonizing over sleeping with her, days of not knowing how *she* felt about it, bubbled to the surface and his temper exploded. "That was the best damned sex I've ever had!"

Stunned silence echoed through the cab. *Way to go. Now Shannon can drag you around by your ears and stomp you flat.*

"Me, too."

Her quiet admission knocked the fight out of Johnny and he expelled a long breath.

"So where do we go from here?" she said.

"Nowhere."

Her stare burned the side of his neck.

"I crossed the line with you, Shannon. I'm older. I should have known better. You had too much to drink that night and—"

"Three beers. I knew exactly whose clothes I was taking off."

If his face grew any hotter it would melt. "Doesn't matter. I've known you forever and I shouldn't have taken advantage of you."

"Maybe I took advantage of you."

He glanced across the seat. Was she for real?

"Are you being stupid about this because you regret breaking up with Charlene?"

Stupid? "I'm over Charlene."

"Then why are you acting like what we did was a first-class felony?"

"You're practically my sister!"

"I am not your sister, so you better not use that lame excuse."

"Lame? I cleaned your skinned knees and—"

"You put bandages on them, too." She laughed.

"It's not funny, Shannon. You sat at our dinner table more often than you sat at your father's."

"That may be true, but I'm no longer a little girl. I'm all grown up. Didn't you notice that in the shower?"

Hell, yes, he'd noticed.

"Are you worried about what my father might think?" she asked.

"Aren't you worried?"

"No. My sex life is none of his business."

"Are you going to tell him?" If Johnny lost his job, he'd have to come clean with his brothers about the farm's financial troubles.

"I'm not going to tell my father." She tapped her nail against the armrest on the door and the clicking sound grated on his nerves. "So you want to forget about sleeping together and call it a mistake?"

"I think that's best, don't you?"

"I suppose."

This conversation hadn't been as tough as he'd imagined it would be. If they'd had this talk the day after they'd slept together they might have spared themselves—at least him—all this anxiety. "Okay, then. We'll forget about it."

She snorted. "Already done."

This was going to be a hell of a long day.

"THERE YOU GO, Rebecca." Shannon handed the auto-graphed program to the little girl with dark pigtails, then watched her walk away with her mother.

"Can I take your picture together?" A man with plas-tic media credentials hanging from his neck motioned to C.J., who stood a few feet away signing his name across the belly of a beautiful blonde bimbo.

"Sure." She nudged C.J. and when he scowled at her, she pointed to the reporter.

"Excuse me," he told the blonde, then pulled Shannon close. As soon as the camera flash went off, he removed his arm. Another fan shouted, "Wait, I want a picture!" From then on it was a steady stream of fans snapping photos of her and C.J.

Shannon glanced at Johnny, who stood nearby watch-ing. A short while ago he'd looked bored to death, but right now wisps of steam leaked from his ears. *Good.* It would serve him right if he was jealous after insisting it had been a mistake for them to sleep together.

She might be nine years younger than Johnny, but she wasn't so naive that she hadn't noticed the chemistry be-tween them. It ticked her off that he didn't want to admit they'd rung each other's bells.

"How about a kiss!" someone in the crowd yelled.

C.J. quirked an eyebrow.

Oh, what the heck. She lifted her chin and C.J.'s mouth drew closer. Just when she felt his breath caress her face, a hand spun her around.

"Isn't it time for Rodriguez to get ready for his bull ride?" Johnny glared at C.J.

If having sex with her had been no big deal, Johnny sure had a funny way of showing it.

C.J. whispered in her ear. "I don't think he's playacting anymore."

"Johnny's right." Shannon shoved C.J. "Your ride's coming up."

"I'm winning this one for Shannon," C.J. boasted, and the fans shouted their encouragement as he and Johnny headed to the cowboy ready area.

When they arrived behind the chutes, Shannon checked the JumboTron and saw their images displayed across the screen.

"Gonna wish me luck, Cash?" C.J. taunted.

"Break a leg, Rodriguez." A reporter nearby held up his iPhone, recording the exchange.

"Now, boys—" Shannon stepped between the men "—no fighting."

"Stand back, Cash. I'll show you how a winner competes at rodeo."

"Or you'll show me how they lose."

Shannon glanced between the men, unsure if they were serious or pretending.

C.J. spoke to the cowboys by the chute. "Maybe Johnny Cash'll sing the 'Folsom Prison Blues' for us."

"You enjoy making fun of my name, don't you?"

"Well, folks, it looks like C. J. Rodriguez and the Man in Black are quarreling again!"

The announcer's voice startled the cowboys and they stepped apart.

"What's going on down there, C.J.?" the announcer asked from the media booth. All of a sudden a microphone appeared in front of C.J.

"Johnny Cash doesn't want to admit that I'm better at rodeo than he is."

Johnny snatched the microphone from the reporter's

hand. "I'll take you on any day, Rodriguez, just say the word."

"I believe Johnny Cash has just thrown down the gauntlet," the announcer said. "How would you folks like to see these two cowboys square off?"

Thunderous applause and boot stomping filled the arena.

The announcer chuckled. "And the winner gets a date with cowgirl Shannon Douglas."

Shannon sidled up to Johnny. "You don't have to do this."

His smile didn't reach his eyes. "It's just part of the show, right?"

"Let's see who makes it to eight, Rodriguez," Johnny spoke into the microphone. "But we're riding broncs not bulls."

"There you have it, folks, we got us a ride-off today!"

"You didn't bring your gear," Shannon pointed out to Johnny.

"He can use mine." A cowboy in the crowd offered his saddle and rope.

"You sure?" Johnny asked.

"Happy to lend a hand to further the romance," the man said. Another competitor offered his Kevlar vest and spurs, then nodded at C.J. and said, "Put the braggart in his place."

"Sit back and watch the fireworks, folks. We got two cowboys who are going head-to-head in the saddle-bronc event. First up is C. J. Rodriguez." Loud music exploded from the sound system and the JumboTron showed several cowboys riding broncs then faded to black.

"As many of you know, cowgirl Shannon Douglas suffered a bad wreck back in August on a bull named Heat

Miser. A broken leg has put her competition with C.J. on hold for a while." After the fans honored Shannon with a round of applause the announcer said, "Check out the JumboTron, folks."

Good grief. Footage from Johnny and C.J.'s fight behind the chutes in Yuma played across the screen, inciting a frenzy of catcalls and whistles. "Looks like Johnny Cash and C. J. Rodriguez have a score to settle."

Shannon gritted her teeth to keep from protesting the way this love triangle was being played out before rodeo fans. *Do it for the title.* She was close enough to achieving her dream of winning Cowgirl of the Year that putting up with a little sexist behavior wouldn't kill her.

"C. J. Rodriguez is riding Big Bang, a bucker from the Pine Top Mountain Ranch in Colorado."

Standing in the shadows, Shannon watched C.J. prepare for his ride. He was agitated—served him right. Now he knew how she'd felt when he'd baited her at the rodeos. C.J. glanced up and made eye contact with Shannon. She dutifully waved, then he brazenly blew her a kiss with his free hand. The crowd went nuts.

The gate opened and Big Bang went to work. C.J. hadn't ridden a lot of broncs the past few months because of their bull riding competition and she noticed his spurring was off. By the third buck he was slipping in the saddle. The fourth buck sent him flying through the air. C.J. landed hard and was slow to get up, but he bowed toward the stands and the fans applauded his effort.

"Up next is Johnny Cash, coming out on Mud Bog, a four-year-old bucker from the Carlisle Ranch outside Payson, Arizona."

Shannon inched closer to the chute, not caring if fans believed she favored Johnny over C.J. She was worried about Johnny—he hadn't rodeoed in a long time—since he'd begun working full-time at the Triple D four weeks ago. If he hurt himself and couldn't keep up with ranch chores, she didn't want to be the one to tell her father how he'd gotten injured and why.

She climbed the rails next to Johnny as he worked the rope around his hand. "Are you sure you want to go through with this?"

"Don't have much choice, do I?"

She lowered her voice, so the cowboys by the chute didn't hear her. "You can scratch. A ride-off wasn't part of the deal Dynasty Boots offered you."

"I'm not scratching. Rodriguez's head is already too big for his body."

Men.

"Watch me kick his ass."

Or get your backside stomped flat. "Do you know anything about this horse?" she asked.

"He bucks high and tight and spins left." A cowboy Shannon didn't recognize spoke from behind her. "I rode Mud Bog in Houston earlier this year."

Before she'd prepared herself, Johnny nodded to the gateman and the chute opened. The bronc vaulted into the arena and did exactly what the cowboy had warned— Mud Bog bucked high and tight twice, then twirled left and repeated the action. Johnny hung on, his spurring mediocre at best.

Shannon held her breath, wondering if the gut-tugging anxiety she felt was anything close to what Johnny had experienced when he'd watched her leave the chute on Heat Miser. Eyes glued to the action she ticked off the seconds in her head. Johnny fell out of the saddle just as the buzzer sounded. She doubted the judges would give him credit for the ride.

"Well, folks, Johnny Cash almost made it to eight. Looks like he and Rodriguez will have to fight it out another day."

Shannon watched Johnny leave the arena, noticing the limp in his stride. "You okay?" she asked when he stopped to remove his gear.

"Fine." Sensing he needed some space, she backed off and waited for the hoopla to die down.

"Wouldn't hurt for you to act like you prefer me over Cash," C.J. grumbled as he approached her.

"I doubt you're jealous, not with all the buckle bunnies vying for your attention," she said.

"That's different."

"You only have to do this one more time before I'm back in the arena competing against you."

"You think you're ready to take me on again?"

"I will be."

"Coming back from injuries isn't easy. Been there, done that," C.J. said.

"Don't worry. I intend to give you a fight right down to the finish."

He inched closer and touched her arm. "You do realize that there's no way I'm letting you win this competition between us."

"You don't have to let me win because I'm taking the victory."

"Why is beating a man in bull riding so important to you?" he asked.

"I'm not in this to prove I'm better than you or any man. I'm doing this because I want the title of Cowgirl of the Year."

"If all you care about is a damned title then you could have picked a less dangerous event to go after it."

"Then the title wouldn't mean as much, would it?"

"You're one crazy woman." He and Shannon exchanged smiles, which drew stares, including Johnny's.

Johnny walked up to Shannon. "We done here?"

"I believe we are," she said.

"Nice try, Cash." C.J. lowered his voice. "Next time I'll beat the buzzer."

Shannon glanced between the men. "There won't be a next time."

"You protecting lover boy?" C.J. asked.

"I don't need anyone's protection." Johnny glared at Shannon, then shifted his dark gaze to C.J. "I'll take you on anytime anywhere. Just name the rodeo."

"Hey, hold up here." Shannon placed her hands against both men's chests and straightened her arms, pushing them farther apart. "There will be no more ride-offs."

"You letting her do all your talking for you, Cash?"

"C.J., stop it. Johnny's working at the Triple D. He can't afford to get injured."

"Sleeping with the boss's daughter, are you?"

Johnny moved Shannon out of the way and took a swing at C.J., but the bull rider ducked and Johnny stumbled forward.

Not again.

After regaining his balance Johnny tackled C.J., who'd become distracted by a buckle bunny. "Keep your hands off Shannon, got that?" Johnny growled.

C.J. rolled on top of Johnny. "She was mine first."

Two cowboys pulled them apart and Shannon said, "Let's go, Johnny." She turned away but C.J. caught her around the waist and dipped her over his knee, then ducked his head and skimmed his lips across her cheek. "That ought to piss off the Man in Black until next time." C.J. set her on her feet and walked away, catcalls and whistles echoing in the air.

Johnny took Shannon by the elbow and escorted her toward the exit. Once outside in the parking lot she made a move to pull her arm free but Johnny held tight. When they arrived at his truck he backed her against the door and kissed her—not a soft, gentle kiss. A passionate, breath-stealing kiss.

His mouth worked her lips open and he thrust his tongue inside. When he pulled away, he said, "Get in."

Feeling slightly woozy, Shannon obeyed without protest, thinking that this love triangle might be a lot more fun than she'd imagined.

Chapter Eight

Sunday morning Johnny dropped the last hay bale off the back of his truck, then sat on the tailgate and took a swig of water as the herd made its way toward the feed. He loved fall in Arizona. The third weekend in October had arrived and with it, a dip in temperatures. Mornings started out in the mid-fifties while afternoon temperatures reached the eighties—perfect weather for working outdoors.

And preparing for the pecan harvest.

After the Winslow rodeo Dynasty Boots had sent Johnny a check for half the five thousand they'd promised him for playing his part in the fake love triangle between him, Shannon and Rodriguez. Johnny had used the money to make a down payment on the farm's back taxes.

He wasn't looking forward to the next rodeo, whenever that was. Acting a fool had been too easy, considering that his jealous feelings were one hundred percent authentic and not make-believe. His brain insisted there were too many logical reasons he and Shannon shouldn't be together, but every time Rodriguez so much as looked at her, Johnny felt the urge to claim Shannon as his. None of it made sense.

He pushed thoughts of Shannon aside. He had more

pressing problems to address. He'd yet to lease the pecan orchards to an agricultural company, but at least he'd found a harvesting company willing to bring in this year's crop. Now he had to find markets to sell the nuts. If he didn't, he and his siblings would be eating a whole lot of pecan pie. The thought of the sweet dessert triggered a trip down memory lane.

September through November had been busy months on the farm. He and his brothers would pitch in doing odd jobs for their grandfather while migrant workers harvested the nuts. After his grandfather died, they'd leased the orchards to big companies who brought in huge machines that eliminated the need for laborers to gather the nuts from the ground and clean up the dead branches and debris. A process that used to take a month and a half now took a week from start to finish.

Shoving aside his nostalgic feelings he shut the tailgate and drove back to the ranch house to help Clive with Odyssey—the horse was making progress but not fast enough for the boss's liking.

When he pulled up to the barn, he noticed a familiar blue Toyota Prius parked in the driveway—Shannon's physical therapist had been working with her every day.

"Clive, you in here?" Johnny called when he entered the barn. No answer. He returned his tools to the equipment room and had almost made it to the foreman's cabin when the front door of the main house flew open. Clive raced down the porch steps and made a beeline for the barn.

"Clive!" The boss kept walking.

Johnny hurried after him. "What's the matter?"

"I can't take it anymore."

"Take what?"

Clive's hand shook when he ran his fingers through his hair. "My daughter," he said, then disappeared into the barn.

Even though a voice in his head said it wasn't any of his business, he went up to the main house. When he stepped inside, he noticed Hank's scruffy tail sticking out from under the sofa in the parlor.

"What are you hiding from?" The dog's tail swished then disappeared from sight when a shrill scream rent the air.

Johnny leaped forward, taking the stairs two at a time. He raced to Shannon's bedroom, raised his hand to knock, then cursed his stupidity and barged inside.

At first his mind had trouble processing the scene before him. Shannon lay on her back in the middle of the bed and a short, stocky man with bulging biceps crouched over her, his meaty hands holding her left leg against his chest while he pressed the ball of Shannon's foot toward her.

"Harder," the goon grunted.

Eyes squeezed closed Shannon clutched the comforter and screamed again. The hulk twisted her foot sideways and she cried out.

"Stop!" Johnny pushed the man away from Shannon. "Ease up, buddy." He glared at the therapist. "You're hurting her!"

"It's not supposed to feel good." The gorilla repositioned Shannon's leg against his chest. "One more time. Push."

Shannon complied, grimacing.

"Wimp." The man hopped off the bed and held out

his hand to Johnny. "Rory Davis. Make sure the next two hours she alternates between ice and heat on her Achilles tendon."

Johnny opened his mouth to protest but Rory talked over him.

"She can take up to three anti-inflammatory pills at a time but no more than that." Davis wrapped an ace bandage around Shannon's puffy foot and ankle. "Make sure she keeps a pressure bandage on at all times except when she showers. And she's got to keep the leg elevated when she's lying down."

"Hey, I'm not a two-year-old." Shannon scowled. "I can take care of myself."

The therapist slung his duffel bag over his shoulder. "See you next time." Then he was gone, leaving Johnny dazed and wondering what the hell had just happened.

Shannon swung her legs off the bed and sat up. Sweat dripped down her temples and pain lines marred her forehead. She limped over to the chair by the window and propped her leg up on the stool in front of it. "Can you hand me the ice pack in that cooler?" She pointed to the floor by the bed.

Johnny retrieved the pack and she slid it beneath her calf.

"Thanks." Breathing hard, she wiped the perspiration from her face and that's when he noticed the tear clinging to her lashes.

"You're crying."

She stared at him defiantly. "No, I'm not."

"Yes, you are." He held out a tissue from the box on the nightstand and said, "Why was that guy—"

"Rory."

"—being so rough with you? For God's sake, he could break your bone all over again." The urge to hug her was strong so Johnny backed up several steps and stood in the middle of the room. "You should change therapists."

"Rory's the only one who works with athletes and he's covered by my insurance." She grimaced. "I'm tired. Go away."

Johnny had always admired her toughness and determination, but after watching the torture she'd gone through a few minutes ago he feared she was her own worst enemy. "Can I get you anything to eat or drink before I head out?"

"No, thanks." She forced a shaky smile. "Johnny?"

"What?"

"Is my father outside?"

"He's in the barn."

Her gaze swung to the window. "The doctor said I have a buildup of scar tissue on my Achilles tendon and it's going to take longer to break it down."

"Then go slow with your rehab. You could do more damage to your leg if you push yourself too hard." He walked to the doorway and whistled. Hank's nails clicked against the wood stairs, then the dog trotted into the room and went straight to Shannon's chair and sat by her side.

"Hey, boy." She scratched the hound's ears.

"He was hiding under the couch."

"Did all that racket scare you?"

The dog's tail thudded against the floor.

Without taking her eyes off Hank she said, "As soon as I'm finished icing my leg, I'll talk to my dad."

"Good luck," he said, and left the room. He didn't

want to be anywhere nearby when Shannon and her father went at it again over rodeo.

SHANNON ENTERED THE BARN and paused, allowing her eyes to adjust to the dimness. It was quiet and she wondered if her father had gone for a horseback ride. The expression on his face when she'd screamed was much like Johnny's had been a short time later—pasty-white. She hated that her therapy was upsetting her father and wanted to reassure him that she was going to be okay.

"Dad?"

"Back here in the tack room."

She moved through the barn, consciously making an effort to conceal how bad her limp was. She found her father sitting on a stool, rubbing linseed oil into a bridle. "Can we talk?"

He motioned to the chair in the corner and she sat down. "You okay?" she asked.

He didn't answer.

"It sounded worse than it was."

He kept his eyes on the bridle. "Fathers shouldn't have to listen to their daughters suffer that kind of pain."

"It'll get better. The first couple of weeks of therapy are the worst." She hoped so anyway, because she couldn't bear the thought of hurting like this for months on end.

"I don't get it, Shannon."

"Get what?"

"Why you're putting yourself through this."

"I've got to get back to rodeo sooner rather than later or I'll lose my edge and it'll be no contest come January when C.J. and I compete in our final ride-off."

"Your leg might not ever be a hundred percent again."

She wished her father would have a little faith in her. "I'm not letting a broken leg end my rodeo career."

"It's my fault, isn't it?" He stared at her as if she were a stranger. "I made you decide you wanted to be as tough as a man."

"I don't want to be as tough as a man. I want to be as tough as *I* can be."

"Don't see much difference." He cleared his throat. "Do you like women? Is that it?"

Shannon groaned. "Are you serious, Dad?"

"You don't bring any fellas home and you didn't date in high school."

"I admit I'm a tomboy but that doesn't mean I haven't…" She was not going to discuss her sex life with her father. "I like boys, okay?"

"Then what's driving you, daughter? You were lucky you walked away from that crash in Yuma with only a broken leg and a concussion."

"I'm so close to winning a title. I might never get this close again."

"Then it's Arlene's fault."

"Arlene? You mean Mom?"

"If your mother hadn't skipped out on the family, maybe you'd have grown up wanting to be a girl instead of a boy."

"I don't want to be a boy. I'm very happy being a girl." Who knew what would have happened if her mother had decided to remain with the family? But what was done was done.

"Maybe I should have married again, but I kept thinking Arlene would come back."

This was the first time she'd heard her father say such a thing about her mother. "Did you love her?"

"Any love I felt for her died when she walked out on you as a baby." He frowned. "What mother leaves her children and never has contact with them again?"

"I don't know, but Matt, Luke and I had you, Dad."

"I wasn't enough." His chest shuddered as he expelled a deep sigh. "I had no idea what to do with a girl." He waved a hand before his face. "When you fell into step with Matt and Luke, I just treated you all the same."

"Stop beating yourself up over how you raised me. You did the best you could." Fearing he'd only become more upset, she didn't dare tell him how much it bothered her that she'd grown up without a mother.

"You raised me to be a competitor just like you and my brothers. You were all good at rodeo and won titles." She smiled. "I want one, too. It's as simple as that."

"What happens if you don't win a title?" he asked.

"Then I keep at it. I'm a Douglas and Douglases aren't quitters, right?" Shannon didn't give her father a chance to answer. She got up from the stool and gave him a hug. "Everything's going to be fine. Don't worry."

Eyes stinging, she left the barn and returned to the house to take a nap and forget that she and her father had more in common than rodeo talent—neither had gotten over Arlene's abandonment.

FEAR.

Shannon could smell it in the dust that swirled in the air when Heat Miser pawed the dirt in the chute.

Warmth.

A burning sensation singed the inside of her thighs when she settled on the bull's back.

Pain. As if someone stabbed the tip of a hot poker

into her leg, each jab caused the calf muscle to tighten and twist.

The din from the rodeo fans chanting Heat Miser's name pressed in on her from all sides and she could barely hear herself think. Why were they cheering for the bull? They were supposed to be cheering for her.

She gazed across the arena at the scorers' table. The three men pointed at her and laughed as if they knew how the ride would end before the gate even opened.

Her gaze locked onto the trophy in the center of the table—a tall, gold-plated cowgirl riding a bull, her right arm high above her head, her long ponytail flying out behind her. That trophy belonged to her.

She dropped the end of the bull rope over Heat Miser's shoulder, and a cowboy reached under the bull's belly with a hook and snagged the end, then handed it back to her. Sweat dampened her armpits. The air in the arena began to evaporate and each time she sucked in a breath, less and less oxygen filled her lungs until she felt dizzy and the cowboys leaning over the chute wavered before her eyes.

She shook her head to clear her vision and realized her mistake. The rodeo worker opened the gate and Heat Miser vaulted into the arena before Shannon had a secure grip. She managed to hang on through the first buck but began sliding when the bull spun. She tried to release the rope, but her glove got caught in the rigging and she hung by her arm alongside the bull. The tips of her boots dragged across the ground as she tried to free her fingers.

A cowboy on horseback approached and cut the rope. Shannon dropped to the dirt but quickly got to her knees. She took one step then froze. Heat Miser had stopped

bucking and stared her down. Sitting on the ground between them was the Cowgirl of the Year trophy.

Heat Miser pawed the dirt.

Back off, big guy. She glanced sideways—where were
the bullfighters? Where were the fans? The bleachers
were empty.

It was just her and Heat Miser. The bull bellowed and
began to charge. Shannon raced toward the trophy intent
on getting to it first, but her leg buckled and she went
down. Heat Miser kept coming—he lowered his head
and tossed the trophy into the air, then he kept coming...
straight for her.

Shannon's eyes popped open and she sat up in bed,
gasping for air. The nightmare was growing worse. It
had begun when she'd come home from the hospital—
blurry scenes of past bull rides. Not until she'd gotten the
cast off her leg had the nightmare become more vivid.

She had to get a handle on her fear before it robbed
her of a national title. Maybe it was time she got on the
mechanical bull. Once her body went through the mo-
tions of a bull ride, her subconscious would accept that
she knew what she was doing and that knowledge would
keep the demons at bay when she slept. She'd ask for
Johnny's help in moving the machine out of the storage
shed, but first she needed a shower to rinse off the fear
that clung to her skin.

JOHNNY DROPPED A LOAD of dirty jeans into the washer,
added detergent and closed the lid. There were lots of
perks to living alone—he didn't have to fight six siblings for the washing machine. After numerous brawls
over the appliance, he'd assigned his brothers and sister a day during the week to do their wash. Now that he

lived alone, he had to remind himself that he could clean his clothes any day of the week—not just Sunday nights.

When he stepped from the small room Shannon stood in the kitchen. Startled, he asked, "What's wrong?"

"Nothing. I knocked twice but you didn't answer the door, and—" she pulled a chair out from the table and sat "—I needed to get off my leg."

"Can I get you a drink?" he asked.

"No, thanks." She smiled and Johnny's pulse raced. From across the kitchen he caught the scent of her perfume and suddenly the cabin, which he'd believed had been plenty big enough, felt cramped. He admitted that Shannon had bruised his ego when they'd discussed their one-night stand in Gila Bend and she hadn't protested much when he'd insisted that night had been a mistake. The least she could do was mope around the ranch, instead of focusing on rodeo and acting as if she didn't give him or what they'd shared a passing thought.

He removed a frying pan from the cupboard next to the stove then two plastic food containers from the fridge. "I'm reheating leftover spaghetti for supper. You want some?"

She shook her head. "It's seven-thirty. Why are you eating so late?"

"Took me longer than I'd expected to muck the stalls this afternoon." At the last minute, Clive had backed out of helping Johnny, claiming he needed to run an errand in town. Ever since his boss had heard his daughter scream during her physical therapy session, he didn't stick around when Rory showed up.

Johnny dumped the spaghetti into the frying pan, lowered the heat and leaned a hip against the counter, studying Shannon. Sooner or later she'd get to the reason she'd stopped by. In the meantime he'd ask a question that had been burning in the back of his mind since she'd begun therapy two weeks ago. "I didn't know physical therapists made house calls on weekends."

"My insurance covers twenty sessions. It's up to me how far apart to space them and since Dynasty Boots has me competing in Chula Vista at the end of November, Rory's agreed to work with me every day until I hit my limit."

"How swell of *Rory*." Johnny ignored the sudden hardening of his stomach muscles. Shannon was an attractive woman—it wasn't any surprise that *Rory* was willing to make time for her every day.

"I need your help," she said.

"What kind of help?" He stirred the noodles.

"I'd be grateful if you'd pull the mechanical bull out of the storage shed and put it behind the barn."

"Are you crazy?" He whirled so fast sauce flew off the spoon and splattered the floor. Hank got up from his bed and licked the spots clean.

"No, I'm not crazy. I need to practice," she said.

"You haven't finished your physical therapy."

"My Achilles tendon doesn't need to be a hundred percent to practice."

"What if you fall and reinjure the tendon? Then what?"

"That's not going to happen." She got up from the table. "If you don't want to help, I'll ask someone else."

Probably Rory. "I'll take care of it." He'd get one of his brothers to come over and help him.

"Thanks." She limped to the door. "By the way, Dynasty Boots wants you and me and C.J. to attend the Douglas Rodeo the first weekend in November."

"That's next Saturday." Relief mixed with dread filled

Johnny. Relief that he'd earn another twenty-five hundred dollars, and dread that he had to put up with Rodriguez and his ego again.

"They want us there by noon," she said.

"Shannon."

"What?"

"How'd the talk with your dad go?"

"Same as always." She opened the door.

"You're his daughter. He's going to be overprotective."

"What about you?" she asked. "How do you feel about me rodeoing?"

"My feelings don't matter. You're not my sister, daughter or wife."

"If I was one of those things?"

"Then I'd tell you to quit the sport and not put yourself in any more danger."

"You don't believe in me, either."

"It doesn't matter what I believe." If he really felt that way then why did his chest physically ache when he imagined Shannon on the back of a bull?

"You're right." Her chin jutted. "Your opinion doesn't matter."

Ouch.

Then she was gone.

Johnny stared at the leftovers in the frying pan and lost his appetite. He chucked the food into the garbage, washed the pan, then sat down and called Mack. No answer—his brother was probably busy at the dude ranch.

Next, he dialed Buck. Same result.

Will's phone went straight to voice mail.

Porter's phone rang and rang without connecting to voice mail.

Well, damn. The only one left was Conway—Mr. Romeo. Conway was more concerned with having a good time than doing anything productive.

"Hey, big brother. What's up?"

Johnny heard music in the background. "It's Sunday night. Are you at a bar?"

"The Wet Whistle's open and I'm hoping to get lucky on the Sabbath and find *the one,*" he said.

Conway was always on the lookout for *the one.* "I need a favor," Johnny said.

"When?"

"Tonight. I need your help at the ranch." Dead silence. "You there?"

"Didn't you hear what I said?" Conway asked.

"I heard. Forget about the girl. I need your help."

"You need to get laid, Johnny. You've been in a crappy mood ever since you broke up with Charlene."

"Are you helping me or not?" After all he'd done for his brother through the years…

"Yeah, okay. I'll leave the bar now," Conway said.

While waiting for his brother to arrive, Johnny finished his laundry, changed the linens on the bed, cleaned the toilet, then took Hank outside and sat on the porch.

At a few minutes before ten o'clock Conway's truck turned onto the road leading to the ranch house.

"Thanks for coming," Johnny said when his brother got out of his truck. "Sorry if I derailed your love life tonight." He cut across the drive and Conway fell in step beside him.

"Are the rumors true?" Conway asked.

"What rumors?"

"That you're romantically involved with Shannon? Is that why you broke up with Charlene?"

Johnny skidded to a halt. "Who told you I was involved with Shannon?"

"Hell, Johnny. Your brawl with Rodriguez at the Winslow rodeo is all anyone's talking about on the circuit."

"I'm not in a relationship with Shannon and she's not the reason I ended things with Charlene."

"But the brawl did happen?"

Was that humor he heard in his brother's voice? "It's not what it seems." He opened the storage shed next to the barn. "There's an old set of rolling dollies in the back. See if you can find them."

"Sure, make me search through the dark and get bit by a spider." Five minutes later, Conway had found the dollies and they shoved them into place. Carefully they rolled the machine out of the shed, then pushed it behind the barn.

"Crap, that thing is heavy." Conway took off his hat and wiped his shirtsleeve across his brow. "So?"

"So thanks for your help."

"Ha, ha. What's up with you and Rodriguez fighting over Shannon?" When Johnny remained silent Conway asked, "Have you slept with her?"

His brother wouldn't drop the subject—no wonder when his day-to-day life consisted of rodeo and female drama. Too bad Johnny knew how to shut Conway up. "You figure out yet what you're going to do with your life?"

"Not you, too. Buck got all over me yesterday about finding a permanent job just because I asked if it was all right to bring Cindy Packard back to the bunkhouse to watch a movie."

"It's time for you to pull your weight." They walked back to the cabin.

"You know what I think?" Conway said. "You guys ride my ass because you're jealous of me."

Johnny chuckled. "Jealous?"

"You guys wish women fawned all over you like they do me. I can't help it if I'm the best-looking Cash brother." He got behind the wheel. "Watch yourself with Rodriguez. He's a ladies' man. If he wants Shannon, he'll get her."

Over my dead body.

"Thanks for driving all the way out here to help tonight."

"Dixie said she wants a big Thanksgiving celebration this year. Will bought a deep fryer and she's cooking three turkeys."

"Tell Dixie to count me in for dinner."

As Conway drove off, Johnny thought he had little to be grateful for this Thanksgiving—then an image of him and Shannon in bed together at the Hacienda Motel flashed before his eyes and he changed his mind—he did have one memorable experience to be grateful for.

Chapter Nine

"Shannon!"

Oh, boy. What had lit her father's pants on fire this morning? Bracing herself, she limped out of the kitchen. Her father stood by the front door—head lowered, nostrils flaring.

"What's the matter?" she asked.

"You know darn well what's wrong."

Feigning ignorance, she said, "No, I don't."

His cheeks puffed out, and then a gust of air escaped his mouth. "Follow me." The front door slammed behind him.

Shoring up her defenses, Shannon trailed after him. Halfway across the drive she saw a hay bale fly out of the door at the top of the barn. The feed landed on the ground near a flatbed trailer. As she drew closer, she got a better view of Johnny, wearing only jeans and boots. When he tossed another bale, the glistening muscles across his chest and shoulders rippled. Two more bales sailed through the air before he saw her.

He stared, chest heaving from exertion. She tried—really tried—to keep her gaze on his face, but her eyes drifted lower and lower to where a thin line of dark hair began below his belly button and disappeared beneath the waistband of his jeans. When she found the strength to tear her gaze from the crotch of the threadbare denim, she noticed his grin. So what if he'd caught her ogling him—it was no secret that she liked his body. She turned the corner of the barn and found her father waiting next to the mechanical bull.

"What's the meaning of this?" He jabbed his hat toward the machine.

She heard the creaking of the hayloft door above her head but resisted glancing up. "I need to practice before I compete at the end of November." And she hoped the more she worked out, the weaker her nightmares would grow until they eventually disappeared.

"You haven't finished your physical therapy."

"Rory said my leg is fine." She crossed her fingers behind her back and hoped she wouldn't get caught in the lie.

"You're still limping." Her father's pacing plowed a furrow in the dirt. "Tendons take time to heal. If you push yourself too soon, you'll do more damage."

She appreciated that he worried about her safety and health, but the sooner he accepted that she wasn't giving up her hunt for a title, the better for both of them. "What happened to the man who told me to stop bellyaching and get back on my horse after I'd fallen off and skinned my knees?"

A tense thirty seconds passed before her father broke eye contact. "I've never hated your mother as much as I do right now." He disappeared into the barn, leaving Shannon shaken.

She glanced up at the hayloft seeking reassurance from Johnny, but the doorway was empty.

FRIDAY MORNING JOHNNY dropped a large piece of plywood on the ground and dust billowed into the air. He and Clive had finally cured Odyssey of his fear of loud noises and now Clive had asked him to work with a different gelding on loading. The horse was terrified of trailers and refused to leave the corral. He approached Gentle Ben, took the reins and coaxed him toward the plywood, but the horse backed away. Johnny would have to sweeten the lesson. He went into the barn for a bucket of grain.

When he returned to the pen, he spotted Shannon in the distance, walking along the road leading to the ranch house. Five days had passed since he and Conway had moved the mechanical bull behind the barn and Shannon had used it every day for hours at a time. Johnny thought she was pushing herself too hard but he kept his opinion to himself. Keeping one eye on her and the other on Gentle Ben, he scattered a handful of grain across the top of the plywood. The horse's nose twitched at the scent. "C'mon, boy." Gentle Ben inched closer and stretched his neck to nibble the treat.

While the horse ate, Johnny watched Shannon. The closer she drew to the house, the more pronounced her limp.

"Shannon, come here a minute," he called out.

Sweat stains marked her T-shirt and her face was flushed from exertion. "Having trouble with Gentle Ben?" she asked when she stopped next to the pen.

"The horse won't load."

"What's up with the plywood?"

"He doesn't like the feel or sound of metal, so I'm using a wood ramp." Johnny motioned to the animal's hooves, which were planted firmly on the edge of the plank.

"What happens when he moves inside the trailer?" she asked.

"I'll cover the metal floor with several inches of hay."

"When do you think he'll be ready to load?"

"Two or three days."

Her gaze drifted to the bucking machine and he said, "I can spot you, if you want."

The furrow across her brow relaxed. "I don't need a spotter."

"I haven't seen you practice your dismount yet."

"Been spying on me, have you?" The corner of her mouth curved up.

It had been difficult not to watch her while he'd mucked stalls in the barn or worked with the horses.

"Okay, sure. I'll try my dismount." She walked away.

Johnny sprinkled more grain on the plywood to keep Gentle Ben busy, then met Shannon behind the barn. "Need a leg up?"

"Nope." She hopped on and found her seat.

Johnny set the level at one. The bull swayed.

"I can handle more power."

He flipped the switch to level two and observed her for signs of pain or distress but his thoughts strayed. The undulating movement of the machine caused her spine to arch, which pushed her breasts forward. He closed his eyes and fantasized about her riding naked, save for her cowboy hat. He envisioned her dewy skin, glistening in the afternoon sunlight, her legs gripping him instead of the...

"Johnny?"

His eyes popped open. "What?"

"Are you okay?"

"Sure, why?"

"I asked you to turn it up a level."

He granted her wish and the machine jerked sharply, causing her to lose her balance. Hanging half on and half off, she struggled to regain her seat. He jumped forward, planting his hands on her rump and pushed her back onto the bull.

"Thanks," she gasped. After a series of erratic spins, she slid again.

This time he couldn't get a solid grip on her fanny and she fell, carrying them both to the ground where she landed on top of him. Her breath puffed across his face and he wanted to kiss her so badly he could taste it. Her softness touched his hardness in all the right places and the contact sent a jolt through his body.

Don't do it.

To hell with right or wrong.

He captured her mouth and thrust his tongue inside, mimicking Shannon's sultry dance on the bull. She sagged against him, her pert nipples zapping his body a second time. He nibbled her lower lip, biting gently until he drew a soft moan from her. Then her fingers found their way inside his shirt and he groaned.

Gentle Ben neighed, the sound bellowing inside Johnny's head like a horn blast. He moved Shannon off of him and crawled to his feet, then helped her to stand. Neither spoke for the longest time, only the bucking machine's grinding gears filled the silence.

"Johnny?" Her green eyes softened and he prayed for the strength to keep from taking her in his arms again.

"What?"

"You're attracted to me."

He didn't bother denying the charge.

"And I'm attracted to you," she said. "So why fight it?"

No matter how much he cared about Shannon and desired her, too much stood in their way. He owed it to his siblings to do everything in his power to hold on to the pecan farm, and right now working for Shannon's father was the only way he could pay the mortgage on the property and keep his promise to his grandfather. Besides not wanting to do anything that might jeopardize his job at the Triple D, he couldn't look past the fact that he disapproved of what Shannon was doing—knowingly putting herself at risk and disregarding the feelings of those who worried about her and loved her.

Whoa. Love? He admitted that he cared about her deeply because she'd been a part of his life for so long and he felt responsible for her welfare. He might even be able to overlook their age difference if she took his feelings into consideration, but the fact that she'd risk her life when the odds were stacked against her proved that she was unwilling to take his feelings into consideration. Falling in love with Shannon when she was determined to put her personal agenda before any future they might have together was a heartache in the making.

"I need to work with Gentle Ben."

"Don't forget the Douglas Rodeo is tomorrow," she said.

How could he forget—another soap opera episode of *How the Rodeo World Turns.*

"I RIDE IN twenty minutes." C.J. stopped in front of the Dynasty Boots stand.

Shannon handed a signed T-shirt to a young teen. When the girl walked off she stared at C.J. "So?"

"Aren't you going to walk me to the chute and kiss me for good luck?"

Aware of onlookers Shannon batted her eyelashes and whispered in C.J.'s ear, "Over my dead body." Resigned to playing the role of the smitten cowgirl, she gathered her personal things and walked with C.J. to the cowboy ready area. As they maneuvered through the swarm of fans at the Douglas Rodeo, she searched for Johnny in the crowd. He'd dropped by the booth a while ago, then had wandered off to who knew where.

A couple of young boys chasing each other cut in front of them and she and C.J. had to stop suddenly. The sharp pain that sliced through the back of her leg stole her breath and she grasped C.J.'s arm to steady herself.

"You okay?" he asked.

"Fine." She forced a smile. "Just playing the adoring cowgirl."

As they walked, Shannon did her best to hide the pain, but her leg felt on fire inside her boot.

"Hey, Shannon…C.J.!" They waited for a reporter to catch up with them. The man held out a mini–tape recorder and his sidekick snapped photos.

"I saw you limping back there." The reporter spoke to Shannon. "Will you be ready to compete against C.J. at the end of the month in Chula Vista?"

"Of course I'll be ready to ride." A cold chill raced down her spine. It wasn't that she couldn't sit a bull and ride, because she could. It was the dismount that worried her. If she landed wrong and reinjured her Achilles, there was a good chance she might not be able to get out of the way of the bull's hooves fast enough, which would end her quest for a national title.

C.J. had a sudden coughing fit and the reporter moved the recorder closer to him. "C.J., is Shannon going to make a comeback and be competitive enough to give you a run for your money?"

"I hope so. I'd hate to win our competition by default, even though I am the better bull rider and all-around athlete." He winked at Shannon.

"That's a pretty bold statement. What do you have to say to that, Shannon?"

"C.J.'s a dreamer. He'll find out sooner rather than later that I'm his reality check."

The cameraman laughed.

C.J. grasped her arm and tugged her after him. "You know, the least you could do is acknowledge my talent," he said.

During the short time they'd been a *real* couple, C.J. admitted no one close to him had ever showered him with praise. "You're right," she said.

He stopped at the chute and put on his Kevlar vest. "I'm right about what?"

"You're one of the better cowboys on the circuit," she said. "But—"

"I knew you couldn't give a compliment without a qualifier."

"Your ego gets in the way of you being the best our generation has ever seen." There, she'd said what all the other cowboys on the circuit thought but wouldn't admit out loud.

"What do you mean my ego's in the way?"

"You're more concerned with your playboy image and entourage of buckle bunnies that half the time you're distracted when you leave the chute." She shook her head. "I can only imagine how many wins you'd rack up if you concentrated on the bronc and not all the other stuff going on in the arena."

He narrowed his eyes. "I'll take your words under advisement, Douglas."

"Ladies and gents, it's time for…"

Shannon blocked out the announcer's chatter and searched for Johnny among the milling cowboys. He was supposed to be hamming it up with C.J. and preparing for his own ride. All of a sudden the rodeo reporter took off running toward a man dressed all in black—*Johnny*.

He stared at her as he strolled closer—the heated look in his eyes reminding her of the night they'd made love.

"Like I said before," C.J. whispered in her ear, "he's not acting."

Music exploded from the sound system and the rodeo announcer continued with his spiel. "There he is, folks. The Man in Black." Applause drew Shannon's gaze to the JumboTron displaying Johnny's image.

"While Shannon Douglas's broken leg mends, Rodriguez is putting his bull-riding on hold and is challenging Cash to a second go-around on broncs."

When Johnny stopped at her side, she said, "Nice outfit." He must have brought the clothes with him and changed in the bathroom.

"Thought I might as well play the part." He nodded to the chutes. "Rodriguez is about to ride."

Shannon hurried to C.J.'s side and scurried up the rails, biting the inside of her cheek when her left leg rebelled. She waved to the fans, then dipped her head toward C.J., her hat blocking the cameras. "Break a leg," she said.

"Real funny." C.J. pulled back and waved his Stetson. The fans cheered and Shannon dropped to the ground.

A moment later the chute door opened and Cyclone went to work. C.J. appeared in control until the bronc dipped his head and whirled right, the move sending his rider flying into the air at the six-second mark.

"Well, that's too bad, folks. Rodriguez almost made it to the buzzer. Looks like it's up to Johnny Cash to see if he can make it to eight on his bronc."

"You ready?" When Johnny didn't acknowledge her question, she asked, "What's the matter?"

"I don't like my draw," he said.

She admired the horse's ebony coat as the rodeo workers loaded him into the chute. "What's wrong with him?"

"There isn't a speck of life in his eyes."

"You'll do fine," she said to reassure herself more than Johnny. Once he got on the horse's back, she climbed the rails after him.

"Next up is the Man in Black…Johnny Cash!" The crowd roared. "Cash is coming out on Serial Killer." More applause. "If this cowboy makes it to eight, he wins the girl today."

The horse hadn't moved a muscle—not even twitched since Johnny sat in the saddle. She dipped her head. "Are you sure you want to do this?"

"I'm sure." He nodded to the gateman and the chute door opened.

Serial Killer was a brute—his bucks and spins calculated to put a cowboy through hell and back. Shannon was mesmerized by the pair—Johnny dressed all in black and the gelding's midnight coloring. The two blended into a giant blur of darkness as Serial Killer threatened to jerk Johnny's arm from its socket. His hat flew off and the bronc stomped it flat. She hadn't realized she held her breath until Johnny catapulted into space, then the air in her lungs exploded from her mouth in a loud gasp. A collective murmur rippled through the stands when his body hit the ground. Before he had a chance to get his legs under him, the horse's hooves came within striking distance of his body.

A pickup man rode into the arena, but it was too late. As Johnny struggled to his feet, Serial Killer's hoof clipped his shoulder, knocking him back to the ground.

The pickup man cornered Serial Killer and released the bucking strap, which calmed the bronc and he trotted out of the arena.

Heart racing, she watched Johnny stagger to his feet.

"Well, folks, Johnny Cash and C. J. Rodriquez didn't win today. Guess they'll continue to fight over Shannon Douglas at the next rodeo."

When Johnny stumbled into the cowboy ready area, clutching his crushed hat, she asked, "How bad are you hurt?" Camera flashes blinded her.

"Shoulder's bruised."

The thought that he could have been seriously injured today propelled her into his arms and she hugged him hard.

Johnny would have hugged Shannon forever but the throbbing ache in his shoulder forced him to release her.

"Hell of a ride, brother." Conway hurried toward him, Porter trailing behind him.

"What are you guys doing here?" Johnny asked.

"We stopped by the Triple D this morning and Clive said you and Shannon had gone to the Douglas Rodeo so we decided to come watch," Conway said.

"Hey, Shannon. How's the leg?" Porter asked.

"Fine, thanks for asking." Shannon excused herself to speak with Dale Carson.

After she walked out of earshot, Conway lowered his

voice and said, "You sure there isn't anything going on between you and Shannon?"

"We're friends, that's all."

Porter laughed. "I might be the youngest brother, but I didn't drop off the turnip truck yesterday. That hug Shannon gave you was more than a friendly squeeze."

Johnny ignored the remark. "Are you guys competing today?"

They both shook their heads no. "How come you didn't tell us you were getting back into rodeo?" Conway asked.

"I'm not. This was a one-time thing."

"Johnny." Dale Carson held out an envelope. "The rest of what we owe you." Carson tipped his hat and moseyed along.

Johnny opened the envelope and checked the bank draft.

"What's that?" Porter nodded to the check.

"Dynasty Boots paid me five grand to pretend that I like Shannon and help stir things up between her and C.J. for the fans."

"That's a lot of money." Porter whistled low between his teeth. "What are you going to do with it?"

"When I filed the taxes on the farm, I took a deduction that I shouldn't have and we owe the government $4,856."

"Why didn't you tell us?" Conway asked.

"Because I'm supposed to take care of the family. Besides, you guys shouldn't have to pay for my mistake."

Conway scowled. "We're a family, Johnny. The farm belongs to all of us."

"I know that."

Porter chimed in. "We should all be involved in making decisions about the farm."

For the first time Johnny saw his brothers as grown men and not siblings who needed protecting. "You're right. From now on, we'll discuss what happens to the farm as a family."

Right then Rodriguez and a few of his rodeo buddies strolled up to Johnny and his brothers. "Well if it ain't the Man in Black and his singing sidekicks Porter Wagoner and Conway Twitty."

Rodriguez's friends laughed.

"Maybe if you sang to the bronc you'd make it to eight," Rodriguez said.

Conway stepped forward. "You lookin' for a fight, Rodriguez?"

"You don't scare me, Conway." Rodriguez narrowed his eyes. "You're just a bad seed your daddy sowed."

Johnny stiffened. Those were fighting words. His brother hated people using Conway Twitty song titles to mock him.

Johnny stepped in front of Conway. "We've already been through the name-calling. You sure you want to go another round?"

"He's sure," Porter said right before his fist connected with Rodriguez's nose. Blood spewed everywhere and an all-out brawl ensued much to Shannon's horror and the delight of the rodeo fans.

Chapter Ten

The scent of roasting turkey and apple pie filled the house early Thanksgiving Day. Shannon's father had left at the crack of dawn to help with ranch chores so Johnny could take the afternoon off to have dinner with his siblings. Shannon intended to surprise her father with a traditional Thanksgiving meal. She hoped her efforts in the kitchen would win her points and ease the tension between them.

She checked the clock—almost noon. While she waited for her brothers to arrive, she set the table. At twelve-thirty her father and Johnny pulled up to the house. "Hey, Dad," she said when her father walked through the front door.

"What's that I smell?" He took off his jacket.

"I made a turkey dinner. Matt and Luke should be here soon." Instead of showing appreciation, her father frowned. "What's the matter?" she asked.

"You didn't tell me you were making dinner."

"I wanted to surprise you."

"You should have told me sooner."

"Why?"

His gaze latched onto the wall. "Fiona Wilson invited me to her home today."

"Fiona Wilson?" The notorious Stagecoach spinster?

"I ran into her outside the barbershop the other week—"

"Are you dating Fiona?"

He scowled. "A man my age doesn't date."

She bit her lip to keep from smiling. "How many times have you run into Fiona in town?"

"A few."

"How old is she?"

"Sixty. What does that have to do with anything?"

"Nothing." Only that she was six years older than Shannon's father. "Would you like to invite her here for dinner?"

His face reddened. "Fiona hasn't cooked for anyone in a long time. I think she's looking forward to serving the meal."

Shannon was disappointed but forced a bright smile. "I'm glad you're going to Fiona's." She retreated to the kitchen, her father right on her heels.

"We're just friends," he said.

"Maybe it will develop into more."

"I'm not looking for anything more." He hovered in the doorway. "I guess now's a good time to tell you that I'll be gone for ten days starting tomorrow."

"Where are you going?"

"On a cruise."

Shannon's eyes widened. "With Fiona?"

He nodded. "She bought the tickets a while back for her and a friend but her friend—" he cleared his throat "—died."

"That's too bad. Where are you cruising to?"

"Hawaii."

"Does Johnny know?"

"I wanted to tell you first. I'll speak to him tonight.

There's a horse I need him to work with while I'm gone." He hovered in the doorway.

"Shouldn't you be getting ready?" *He's nervous.* "Wear your dark green sweater with a pair of tan chinos. That would look nice but casual."

"What shoes?"

"Brown dress boots."

He hurried upstairs and not long after the pipes in the walls rattled when the shower turned on. When Shannon texted her brother Matt that their father wouldn't be joining them for supper he called her.

"Fiona Wilson?" he said.

"I couldn't believe it, either." Shannon poked her head around the kitchen doorway to make sure her conversation remained private.

"Isn't she like eighty years old?"

Shannon laughed. "She's sixty and Dad's nervous. I think it's cute."

"Hey, sis, Luke and I aren't going to be able to make it out to the ranch today."

"Why not?"

"All hell's broken loose with one of our cases and we're driving up to Lake Havasu City to question a man the police took into custody after a traffic stop."

"On Thanksgiving?" She stared at the pile of dirty dishes in the sink. She'd gone to a lot of work to put this meal together.

"The police can only detain the guy for twenty-four hours without charging him and Luke believes he witnessed the suspect we're defending purchase the murder weapon."

Shannon couldn't fault her brothers' devotion to their job and she'd missed her share of family holidays when she'd traveled the rodeo circuit. "Okay, I guess I understand."

Matt offered to stop at the ranch later that night after he and Luke got back into town, but she told him not to bother and to drive safely. As soon as she hung up, she realized she'd forgotten to mention their father's cruise. She'd have to fill them in later, right now the dishes needed to be washed. She worked in the kitchen until she heard her father's footsteps on the stairs.

He'd shaved and combed his hair to the side. She almost didn't recognize him. "You look nice, Dad."

He glanced into the dining room. "When are your brothers coming?"

"They're on their way," she lied. "Say hello to Fiona for me."

He reached for his favorite cowboy hat hanging on the coatrack.

"Leave the hat here."

His hand froze. "You sure?"

"Absolutely." Sweat stains marred the crown and the brim was dingy.

"See you later."

After he drove off, her gaze swung to Johnny's truck parked outside the foreman's cabin. Since she wasn't in the mood to eat turkey alone, she removed the bird from the oven and covered the pan with aluminum foil, then carried it to the foreman's cabin.

When Johnny opened the door, Shannon held out the pan. "Take this with you to the farm."

He grabbed the pan and motioned Shannon inside.

When she slipped past him, she caught a whiff of his cologne and a tiny shiver racked her body. What she really wished for was to spend the afternoon alone with Johnny now that she had the ranch all to herself.

"I made a turkey dinner for my father and brothers, but they canceled on me at the last minute and there's no way I'll eat all this food by myself. I'm sure you and your brothers can polish off another bird."

"You're spending the day alone?" His blue eyes rounded with dismay and Shannon's heart melted. Family meant everything to Johnny and he couldn't possibly understand how her father and brothers had abandoned her on a holiday.

"Dad didn't tell me until a few minutes ago that he got an invite to spend the day with Fiona Wilson."

"I didn't know your father was dating anyone."

"Me neither." Shannon smiled. "Wish everyone a happy Thanksgiving." She walked to the door.

"Wait. You're coming to the farm with me."

"You'll have enough mouths to feed. You don't need another one."

"There's plenty of grub. Besides, Dixie will be upset if you don't come."

"Are you sure I won't be imposing?" Shannon hoped not because she'd love to spend the afternoon with the Cash clan.

"The more the merrier." He glanced at his watch. "Where's Hank?"

"In the house."

"Bring him along."

"Okay. I'll meet you at the truck."

As soon as she left the cabin, Johnny texted Dixie that Shannon was coming with him, then carried the turkey to the truck. Shannon arrived with Hank and they drove to the farm. The smell of turkey and the dog's whining filled the cab. Johnny glanced in the rearview mirror and frowned.

"What's wrong?" Shannon asked.

"Hank's drooling all over the seat." He'd have to use fabric cleaner to get the stains out.

"It was nice of you to let him come. He misses Uncle Roger."

"I'm a sucker for animals. Our grandparents wouldn't let us have a dog growing up."

"Why not?"

"My grandfather accidently ran over the family dog when he was learning to drive and Grandma Ada said he was too heartbroken to ever want another one."

"That's sad. I don't know what I'd have done if I didn't have Hank to keep me company while I was cooped up in the house." After they drove another mile, she said, "Dad told me this afternoon that he's taking a cruise to Hawaii with Fiona."

"When?"

"They're leaving tomorrow. He's going to talk to you tonight about training one of the horses while he's gone."

They arrived at the farm and found a spot among the maze of Cash pickups parked haphazardly about the yard. When Dixie had gotten her driver's license Johnny had assigned his siblings parking spaces in the front yard. The plan had worked for one week and then his brothers had made deals with each other, swapping spots until everyone had subscribed to the whoever-gets-there-first rule.

"Should we chain Hank up outside?" Shannon asked.

He nodded to the bunkhouse where the door stood wide-open. "You can tie his leash to the spigot." While Shannon did that, he carried the turkey inside.

"Johnny's here," Will said when Johnny and Shannon entered the bunkhouse. Several "Heys" echoed after the announcement. His brothers sat on their beds, facing the wall with the TV and watched a football game.

"I'm so glad you came." Dixie set a bowl of mashed potatoes on the table then hugged Shannon.

"Thanks for letting me tag along with Johnny. My dad bailed on me and went over to Fiona Wilson's house."

"I heard Fiona Wilson has a million dollars stuffed inside her mattress," Porter said.

Dixie rolled her eyes. "Gavin, go ahead and watch the game. Shannon will help me with the food."

One of the teams scored a touchdown, and Mack tugged Johnny's shirtsleeve. "What's going on between you and Shannon?" Mack had a sixth sense his other brothers lacked.

"Nothing's going on between us."

"Porter and Conway told me about the fight at the rodeo in Douglas a few weeks ago." Mack stared.

"Rodriguez doesn't know how to keep his mouth shut."

"Getting a little testy, big brother?"

Will jabbed his elbow in Mack's side. "He's got the hots for Shannon."

Scowling, Johnny swung his gaze to Gavin. "You want to add anything to this conversation?"

Gavin shook his head.

"You're robbing the cradle," Mack whispered.

Pissed off that his brother had guessed one of his worries about becoming involved with Shannon, Johnny said, "Shut your mouth, Mack, or I'll shut it for you."

"You guys better not fight today." Dixie glared. "I mean it."

"We won't." Will lowered his voice. "Shannon's not bad-looking for a tomboy."

"She's got pretty green eyes," Porter said.

Johnny regretted asking Shannon to spend the afternoon with his family. "It's none of your business what happens between me and Shannon."

"That means there is something going on between you two," Porter said.

Always the peacemaker, Buck came to Johnny's defense. "Leave him alone, guys."

"Time to eat." Dixie waved her brothers to the table.

Johnny sat at the head and reached for the carving knife.

"Wait," Mack said. "Shouldn't Shannon sit next to you, Johnny?"

"I'm fine right where I am." Shannon avoided eye contact with Johnny.

"Mack," Conway said. "You and Buck shift over one seat and Shannon you sit here." Conway vacated his chair, leaving Shannon no choice but to sit next to Johnny.

When everyone stopped shuffling around, Johnny asked, "Can I cut the turkey now?" The knife barely penetrated the meat. In order to get better leverage, he pushed his chair back and stood, then stabbed the meat fork deeper into the breast and gripped the knife handle tighter. It felt as if he was sawing a two-by-four. Frustrated he pressed the knife down harder and the bird flew off the plate and landed in Will's lap.

"I may have cooked the turkey a little too long," Shannon said sheepishly and everyone laughed.

Will set the bird on the counter. "After dinner I'll cut off some of the meat and give it to Hank as a treat."

Dixie fetched another turkey from the counter and set it in front of Johnny. "Try this one." She winked at Shannon.

Johnny's knife cut easily through the tender meat and in a matter of minutes everyone's plate was piled high with food.

"Before we say grace, I have an announcement to make." Dixie shared a smile with Gavin, then held up her water glass.

"Spit it out, Dix, before the food gets cold," Porter said.

"Gavin and I are expecting."

"Expecting what?" Porter asked.

Johnny slapped the back of his brother's head. "A baby, stupid."

"You're pregnant?" Buck asked.

Dixie leaned down and kissed Gavin then said, "We're pregnant."

The brothers congratulated the couple and asked a million questions. Johnny remained silent as he ate, thinking it was odd that his baby sister was the first in the family to have a baby of her own.

Shannon nudged his arm. "Are you excited, Uncle Johnny?"

The sparkle in her green eyes mesmerized him. He couldn't help but wonder what color eyes a child of theirs would end up with—Shannon's deep green or his bright blue or a cross between both.

"Are you okay?" she asked.

"I'm fine," he said, knowing that was the furthest thing from the truth.

"I'm THRILLED FOR YOU, Dixie," Shannon said as they washed and dried the dishes in the kitchen.

"Thanks."

Shannon noticed Dixie's somber face. "You don't look happy for a woman who's been trying to get pregnant for six months."

"I'm excited." Dixie peeled off the latex gloves she wore. "And I'm frightened."

"Of miscarrying again?"

Dixie nodded. "I don't want to lose another baby."

"Your mother had seven children. You'll be fine this time."

"Grandma Ada had several miscarriages," Dixie whispered. "And my mother was born six weeks early."

"Try not to worry. Follow the doctor's orders and leave the rest up to God."

"Gavin's as worried as I am."

"So you two have talked about it?"

"No. He hasn't said a word, but he watches my every move as if he's waiting for me to stumble or double over in pain."

"Gavin was a soldier—it's in his DNA to be overprotective of those he loves." She hugged Dixie. "How far along are you?"

"Seven weeks." Dixie sighed. "There's plenty of time for things to go wrong."

"Stop thinking like that," Shannon said. "Stay positive." Easier said than done. Since her wreck on Heat Miser, she'd had plenty of experience with negative thoughts. Every time she felt a pain in her Achilles tendon it took all her strength to close the door on self-doubts and remain focused on her goal.

"You're right. Worrying will do more harm than good to the baby," Dixie said.

"Once Gavin notices you're at ease with the pregnancy, he'll relax."

"You're a smart woman, Shannon. Thanks for the advice."

"Call me anytime you want to talk. Better yet, stop by the ranch and visit."

"I'm afraid I haven't been a very good friend," Dixie said. "With Christmas around the corner I've been putting in long hours at the gift shop and—"

"I've been just as busy as you."

"Doing what?"

"Practicing on the mechanical bull."

"Why? The Tucson rodeo isn't until January."

"I'm riding this Saturday in Chula Vista."

Dixie pointed to Shannon's calf. "What about your leg?"

"My Achilles is improving every day."

"Is the coast clear?" Johnny's voice drifted through the screen door off the back porch.

"The dishes are all done, no thanks to you or the rest of the boys," Dixie said.

Johnny stepped into the room and Shannon's heart skipped a beat at his intense stare. "Feel like taking a walk through the groves with me?"

"Sure." Shannon ignored Dixie's wink and followed Johnny outside. As they strolled past the barn and along the first row of pecan trees, Shannon conceded that he'd done an admirable job acting as if he'd forgotten sleeping with her at the Hacienda Motel and the heated kisses they'd share since that night. When she inched closer to him, he drifted away. Undeterred, she narrowed the gap and this time when he stepped away he almost got smacked in the face with a tree branch.

"Next Monday a harvesting company is coming out to collect the pecans," he said.

"When your grandfather was alive, all of you helped with the harvest."

"Then we all got jobs and went off to rodeo."

"You couldn't have worked in shifts?" she asked.

"We could have, but Will and Buck jumped ship and confessed that they'd always hated helping with the harvest. So we took a family vote and decided to lease the land to an agricultural company. The Nut and Fruit Grove Company's been great to work with, but after last year's harvest they didn't renew their lease."

"The economy?" Shannon asked.

He stopped next to a tree and examined the leaves on a branch. "They decided to expand their business overseas and cut back on business here in the States."

"Who's going to harvest this year's crop?"

"Henderson Family Harvesters. They travel between southern Arizona and California, bringing in crops for small orchards."

"What will you do with all the nuts?"

"I'm negotiating with a California nut factory." They walked several more yards before he checked the leaves on another tree.

"What are you looking at?" she asked.

"Pecan weevils. The trees need to be sprayed."

"Have you considered selling the land?" she asked.

"I promised my grandfather that I'd keep the orchard in the family."

"Are you busy Saturday?" She swatted at an insect

buzzing near her face. "I thought maybe you could watch me ride in Chula Vista."

Startled by Shannon's question Johnny stopped to gape at her. He hated discussing rodeo with her, because with each passing day it became tougher and tougher to pretend it didn't matter to him that she was determined to ride bulls again when he believed she had no business rodeoing anymore. He wished he hadn't slept with her, because making love had changed everything and he worried their relationship would never return to the way it once had been. Hell, he wasn't even sure he wanted it to.

"What would it take to keep you from riding this weekend?" he asked.

"You surprise me," she said.

"How's that?"

"After the way you stood up to C.J., I never expected that you'd be unsupportive of my efforts."

"You're coming off a broken leg, Shannon."

"My injured leg makes me more determined to beat C.J. in January, so I can clinch the title of Cowgirl of the Year."

"I don't understand you." Was she crazy or just plain stubborn? "You're young and you have your whole life ahead of you."

Shannon propped her hands on her hips. "You never stop, do you?"

"Stop what?"

"Being a parent to everyone."

That didn't sound like a compliment. "I don't know what you're talking about."

"You've been in charge of running your siblings' lives

for so long that you don't know when to back off and let people make their own decisions."

Was that true? He'd guided his brothers and sister through several years without their grandparents, but he'd had no choice. And even when his mother had been alive, she hadn't taken responsibility for her kids. When she left the farm to chase after a man, Johnny had been forced to be the parent.

"I'm sorry. I spoke out of turn," Shannon said. "I know you care about your family and the farm and you believe you know what's best for everyone, but..."

"Go on." He braced himself.

"You know what I think?"

No, but she was going to tell him.

"You don't want to give up control."

"That's not true."

"And you refuse to delegate."

"I can delegate, if I need to." He scowled. "Stop changing the subject. We were talking about you, not me."

"I don't need you to look out for me, Johnny. I've been taking care of myself for a long time."

Shannon wasn't his sister or cousin or niece. But what if she was his... "Would you change your mind about riding if I told you that I care about you?"

"I value your friendship—"

"It's more than that." Johnny stopped walking and tucked a strand of hair behind her ear, his finger lingering against her neck. Then he did what he'd been dying to do since she'd sat next to him at the table and had licked the sugar from the apple pie off her lips. He pulled her close and kissed her. "So?" he said when he ended the kiss.

"So what?"

"Will you scratch your ride on Saturday?"

"Is my father putting you up to this?" she asked.

"No." Johnny grasped her hand and held it tight. "But you're his daughter and he's terrified of losing you."

"If my father was that concerned he should have objected to me riding bulls way back in high school, instead of waiting until I got darn good at the sport." She stepped past Johnny but stopped suddenly when she noticed Conway at the edge of the grove.

"Mind if I have a word with you, Johnny, before I leave?" Conway said.

"He's all yours." Shannon marched off.

When she was out of earshot, Conway asked, "What the hell was that all about?"

"Never mind. What do you want?"

"How come you didn't tell us you hired an outside company to harvest the pecan crop?"

"How'd you find out? I'd planned to tell everyone today."

"The company called Dixie at the gift shop yesterday and asked for directions to the farm. They'll be here Monday morning."

Damn. Johnny had forgotten he'd given the number for Dixie's store as a backup in case the company couldn't reach him.

"What happened to the Nut and Fruit Grove Company?"

Why did Johnny's other brothers not care about what went on with the farm but Conway always needed to know even though he never offered a helping hand? Shannon's accusation that he shouldered all the worry and responsibility in his family popped into his head and instead of telling Conway to never mind again, he said, "The Fruit and Nut Grove Company canceled their lease this past spring."

"Can they do that?"

"They can and they did."

"I thought the company had two years left on the lease."

"They've been renewing the lease a year at a time for a while."

"And you didn't think to tell us?"

"What does it matter now, Conway?"

"It matters because we could lose the farm."

Pissed off that his brother had suddenly shown concern over their inheritance, he snapped. "If you're so worried, you run the farm. You can start by spraying the trees. Weevils are eating the leaves. Once you get that done, you can trim back the branches for the winter. Then next spring, you can supervise the irrigation schedule and the mowing." Johnny stopped talking when he noticed Conway's bug-eyed expression.

Feeling bad that he'd jumped down his brother's throat, he swallowed a curse and walked off. As far as Thanksgivings went—this one sucked.

Chapter Eleven

Early Saturday morning Shannon put her gear bag in the truck and started the engine. She and Johnny hadn't spoken a word to each other since Thanksgiving two days ago and she didn't expect him to step outside and wish her well at the rodeo today.

She'd woken feeling distracted, her thoughts centered on Johnny instead of bull riding. She understood he had a habit of telling others what to do but the sooner he accepted that their sleeping together didn't entitle him to a say in her rodeo career, the better for both of them.

Long ago she'd accepted that her quest for a national title would be a lonely one. Her father and brothers never took time out of their busy schedules to watch her compete, which made Johnny's cold shoulder hurt all the more, because he'd been the one person who'd stood up for her when they'd run into each other on the circuit.

When she reached the highway, she headed west toward California. She'd only driven twenty miles when the calf muscle in her left leg cramped. It seemed that no matter how much time she spent stretching the tendon, relief lasted only a short while. Twice during the trip she pulled off the road and walked off a cramp. By the time she reached the Chula Vista fairgrounds she was in a cranky mood.

Shannon found C.J. signing autographs in the Dynasty Boots publicity tent. "'Bout time you got here." He glanced around. "Where's lover boy?"

"He's not coming today." Shannon smiled for a camera then signed several programs.

"You ready to ride?" he asked.

She smiled. "You're going to lose today."

"No way, Douglas." He waved at a pretty brunette.

After standing for fifteen minutes, Shannon set aside her pen. "I'll be back later."

"Hey, you just got here."

If she didn't walk, she'd end up on the ground, withering in pain. "This is payback for all the times you deserted me at the booth." She took her gear and made her way to the cowboy ready area. She and C.J. were kicking off the rodeo with their rides.

"Ladies and gentlemen, the fine folks at Kemper Rodeo Productions would like to thank you for supporting the Christmas for Kids Rodeo here in Chula Vista, California. Your toy donations will go to needy kids in nearby communities. For more information on this worthy cause…"

Shannon closed her eyes and breathed deeply through her nose. The raw scent of animal, sweaty cowboy and hay combined with the smoky tang of barbecue made her stomach queasy.

I can do this.

Since the morning she'd woken in the hospital after her wreck on Heat Miser, she'd dreamed of this moment. She'd expected to feel some anxiety since she hadn't ridden in almost three months, but the apprehension gnawing away at her insides was far worse than anything she'd dealt with before.

"What's wrong?"

Startled, she opened her eyes and found C.J. staring at her. "Nothing. Why?"

He pointed to the cameramen. "It's showtime."

She swallowed hard and stepped into the light. C.J. slung his arm across her shoulders and they hammed it up for the cameras.

"Heard you drew Slingshot," C.J. said.

Slingshot had been aptly named—most cowboys who rode the bull catapulted through the air before the buzzer. "I can handle him." She carried her gear to the chute.

C.J. nodded to her leg. "You're limping."

"So?" She was tired of people pointing out the obvious.

He bent his head, giving the fans the impression that he was whispering sweet nothings in her ear. "You're not ready to ride, are you?"

"Of course I'm ready." She put on her gear, hoping that if she acted indifferent C.J. would go away. Blood pumping hard through her veins, she rubbed resin on her glove as rodeo workers loaded Slingshot into the chute. The bull reared and the cowboys scrambled for safety. A second attempt proved futile, but on the third try the bull walked into the chute.

Shannon got her first good look at Slingshot—the twenty-three-point bull was gray with black splotches. *I can do this.* Slingshot begged to differ—he kicked out with his back hoof, rattling the chute. She handed her bull rope to a rodeo hand who dropped it into the chute. Before the cowboy snagged the end of the rope to bring it up and around the bull, Slingshot stomped the bell flat.

Heart pounding harder by the second, Shannon's ears began to buzz, but not loud enough that she didn't catch the exchange between onlookers near the chute.

"Ain't never seen a bull act that way."

"He's not givin' an inch today, I'll tell ya that."

"You couldn't get me to ride this monster if you tied three of his hooves together."

"Nah, me neither. Somethin' ain't right with this one."

A wave of nausea hit Shannon hard and she pressed her hand against her stomach, willing herself not to vomit.

"Shannon. You ready?"

Instinct propelled her forward and she scaled the chute, which was trickier than she expected with a sore Achilles tendon. Ignoring the pain spreading through her calf, she paused on the top rail and fussed with her riding glove.

Slingshot kicked out with his hooves, his eyes rolling back in his head. Sweat poured down Shannon's temples and when she took a deep breath, her lungs pinched closed, preventing oxygen from getting in. She steadied herself with a hand on the top rail as the announcer told the fans about her and C.J.'s upcoming ride-off in January. Then he mentioned her bad wreck on Heat Miser this past August and the arena began spinning before her eyes.

"Shannon?"

Her brain told her to release her grip on the rail but for the life of her she couldn't let go and stared at her hand as if it belonged to someone else.

"You okay?"

Move, damn it, move! Nothing.

"Give her some room, guys!"

The cowboys manning the chute backed away, leaving Shannon alone at the top of the rail.

You can do this. Lift your leg.

Before she gathered the courage to move, Slingshot had grown impatient and reared, swinging his head toward Shannon. Stark fear gripped her insides and she released the rail so quickly she lost her balance and crashed to the ground. Stunned she sat in the dirt, heart pounding.

Two cowboys hauled her to her feet and they both spoke at once. She saw their mouths move, but she couldn't hear a word they said.

Then suddenly her eyesight dimmed and she knew if she didn't get out of there, she'd faint. Leaving her bull rope behind she took her duffel bag and walked away, her gaze glued to the exit sign.

JOHNNY PRESSED THE PHONE against his ear and stared down the drive—as if Shannon's truck would appear any second. "How'd she do?"

"You're not going to believe this," Porter said.

Johnny had sent his brother to Chula Vista to keep an eye on Shannon. Even though he'd told himself nothing would go wrong today, for his own peace of mind, he'd wanted someone he trusted at the rodeo—just in case. "Believe what?"

"Shannon scratched."

Stunned, Johnny didn't say a word.

"One minute she was ready to get on the bull, the next she dropped off the rails and walked right out of the arena."

Shoving a hand through his hair, Johnny paced to the end of the porch. Had Shannon lied about her leg being healed enough to compete? "Was she limping?"

"I didn't notice."

"What do you mean you didn't notice? You said she walked away."

"Well, yeah, but—"

"Porter, I asked you to—"

"Hold up, hoss. I did like you said. I just got a little distracted there at the end when—"

"Don't tell me Veronica Patriot was there."

"No, I'm done with that woman."

Johnny wasn't positive his youngest brother had learned his lesson after the rodeo groupie used him to get back at a former boyfriend. "Shannon walked out and no one tried to stop her?"

"'Fraid not. By the way, I picked up her bull rope."

For Shannon to leave the rope behind was a sure sign she'd been rattled. "Are you still at the rodeo?"

"Yep."

"Why didn't you follow Shannon?"

"All you said I had to do was keep an eye on her at the rodeo and report back to you on how she did."

"I gotta go. Thanks for calling." Johnny shoved his cell phone back into his pocket.

Why had Shannon scratched? Was it because of her leg or had she finally come to her senses and admitted her best bull riding days were behind her? He checked his watch—2:00 p.m. He'd have to wait to find out the answers to his questions. In the meantime, he'd work with Clive's newest cutting horse, Bear—named for being a bear to work with.

Before Clive left on his cruise, he'd told Johnny needed the horse trained by the time he got back from Hawaii. He planned to sell the horse to Gary McGovern, a Colorado rancher. If the man was impressed with Bear, he'd told Clive he'd buy several more horses from the Triple D. The boss was counting on Johnny to come through for him, but contrary to the breed's reputation of possessing a well-balanced temperament, Bear loved chasing cattle—without a rider. He had to teach the stubborn sorrel to accept a saddle and a rider all in a week's time.

Inside the barn, he led Bear from his stall and hitched him to the center post. The horse didn't like being tied but Johnny intended to make Bear earn his freedom. Clive had used an old-style general-purpose pad filled with deer hair, so Johnny decided to switch things up and try a Navajo saddle blanket made of wool and double the thickness. He placed the blanket on top of Bear and the horse attempted to rear, but stopped when the rope pulled taut. The blanket fell and when Johnny attempted to straighten it, Bear sidestepped and stomped his hoof. Undeterred, Johnny held the blanket in place.

When Bear stopped rebelling and allowed the blanket to remain on his back, Johnny fetched the saddle. He moved the front cinch, back cinch, breast collar and stirrup out of the way. Standing on the horse's left side, he gently but firmly set the saddle on top of the blanket. The horse tensed when Johnny secured the cinch. After Bear stood still for a while, he loosened the cinch, removed the saddle, then groomed him.

He repeated the process over and over until Bear no longer tensed when Johnny placed the blanket and saddle on him. To reward him for his progress, Johnny fetched a bucket of oats then walked Bear outside to the corral. The horse pranced, stopping every few minutes to eat oats. Johnny returned to the barn to put away the grooming kit when he heard the sound of truck tires. Shannon parked in front of the house. Other than the normal hitch in her gait as she climbed the porch steps, she appeared fine.

When she opened the front door, Hank stepped outside to greet her. After ruffling his fur the pair entered the house and Shannon slammed the door hard enough to rattle the windows.

Johnny wondered what to do next. Should he check on her or give her time to cool off? He voted for checking on her after he took care of Bear. He unsaddled the horse and walked him to his stall, then made sure he had fresh water and feed before going up to the house and ringing the bell.

The door opened. "Go away."

Shannon's puffy eyes and blotchy complexion startled him. "You look like hell."

Self-consciously she ran her fingertips through her shower-dampened hair. "I'm not in the mood for company."

"Too bad." He stepped into the foyer and locked gazes with her.

Shannon was too tired to go nine rounds with Johnny. "Leave me alone."

"What happened in Chula Vista?"

Realizing Johnny wasn't going to honor her wishes and get lost, she retreated to the kitchen and poured herself a glass of iced tea, cursing when she spilled the liquid and it dripped over the edge of the counter.

"I'll get that." Johnny reached for the paper towels hanging from the dispenser on the wall.

"No!" She pushed his hand out of the way and awkwardly bent down to wipe the floor. "I can do it," she insisted, smearing the tea in a circle. When she stood and took a step toward the trash can, her leg buckled and she gasped.

"Shannon—"

She jabbed her finger in his direction. "I can do it, damn it, I can!" Tears burned her eyes. *Don't cry. Don't you dare cry.* The tears came and no matter how fast she wiped them away, more fell. Like a battery-operated toy slowly losing its juice until it came to a complete stop, the anger sputtered out of her, leaving her with a gaping hole inside her chest.

Johnny rubbed the pad of his thumb over her cheek, smearing the moisture across her skin. Her defenses crumbled and she drowned in his blue eyes. "I can do this," she whispered, as if repeating the mantra would somehow make it true.

He hugged her and a voice in Shannon's head insisted she didn't need his sympathy or interference—another voice argued that she did.

She buried her face in the front of his shirt and held her breath, hoping a lack of oxygen would smother her cries. Fat chance. The emotional toll years of hard work, pain, frustration, uncertainty, failure and achievement had taken on her erupted inside her.

The first sob crawled through her body and escaped her mouth in a silent scream. Johnny's hug tightened as if he, too, feared she'd shatter into a million pieces. Her body shook with the force of her sobs and her legs gave out. Johnny sank to the floor with her and leaned against the refrigerator.

She sat between his legs, tucked against his body. At last she felt safe from the world. Her tears went on forever and she had no idea how much time had passed when her wails faded to silent hiccups.

"You ready to talk?" he asked.

Talking wouldn't help. Nothing could change the past or the course she'd set upon.

"I can't help you unless I know what's wrong."

Her heart melted. For as long as she'd known Johnny, he'd been the man everyone depended on in a crisis. He never doubted his ability to handle a problem—he could fix just about anything or find someone who could.

If only sheer willpower could solve her crisis.

"I can sit here all night even if my butt grows numb." The hand on her back moved in a slow circle.

Keeping her face snuggled against the side of his neck, she said, "I scratched today."

"Porter told me."

"Porter?"

"I asked him to go to Chula Vista to—"

"Spy on me?" She smacked his chest with her hand and he grunted.

"I wanted to make sure someone you knew was there in case—"

"I got hurt." She wanted to rail at Johnny for treating her like a child, but she couldn't summon the energy.

"I figured you wouldn't call me after your ride and I wanted to know how you did," he said.

"Now you know."

"You're pushing yourself too hard too soon. Your leg isn't ready—"

"My leg hurt but I could have ridden through the pain."

His fingers tightened against her shoulder. "Then what made you scratch?"

"Fear." The word bounced off the walls, echoing through the kitchen.

"Are you getting enough sleep?" he asked.

"No."

"Dreams?"

"Nightmares."

"How bad?"

"Pretty bad." She sighed. "I thought they'd go away after I began practicing on the bucking machine, but they haven't."

Johnny tipped her chin until their gazes connected. "What are you afraid of?"

This wasn't supposed to become a therapy session, but she was desperate for answers anywhere she could find them. "I'm afraid to do the one thing I'm good at—ride bulls."

"And the nightmares?"

"Began after my wreck on Heat Miser."

"What happens in them?" he asked.

I die. "It's always the same thing—Heat Miser throws me and then he charges."

"Do you remember him stomping your leg?"

"No."

"What about the paramedics putting you into the rescue truck?"

She shook her head.

"I heard somewhere that the brain blocks out the pain so the body can heal," he said.

"And then after I'm healed the brain unleashes the demons to stalk me at night?"

"Can I ask you a question without you getting defensive?" he said.

"Maybe."

"Is the title of Cowgirl of the Year more important than your health and possibly your life?"

She opened her mouth then shook her head. How could she explain something she barely comprehended herself? "Never mind. You wouldn't understand."

"Try me."

"I need to win the title because it will make up for all that I lost when my mother walked out of my life."

"A trophy won't replace your mother, Shannon."

"I won't ever forgive her for abandoning me, but the trophy makes up for the pain of knowing she doesn't love me." Without a mother to guide her, it was no surprise she'd become a tomboy. Rodeo had given her a way to fit in with her brothers and feel as if she belonged in their family. As she grew older and became better at rodeo, she'd been forced to look to bigger challenges to smother the pain.

"I started this journey years ago, Johnny. I have to finish it." Only after winning the title could she finally put her mother's abandonment behind her and move on with her life. She twisted in his lap and stared him in the eye.

"Shannon..." His gaze dropped to her mouth. "This isn't a good idea."

"Shh..." She pressed her finger to his lips. "Let us be, Johnny. Right here. Right now. Just us." She pressed her palm to the back of his neck and coaxed his mouth toward hers. When he didn't resist, she relaxed her guard and allowed herself to feel alive again, knowing that in Johnny's arms she'd forget her fears. Forget scratching at the Chula Vista rodeo. Forget the demons that haunted her day and night.

He stood abruptly, tugging her to her feet. Then he swept her into his arms and carried her upstairs where he tumbled to the bed with her, his mouth seeking hers with urgency. Clothes flew in every direction, and then he took his sweet time teasing her before he sheathed himself.

Wrapping her legs around his waist, she urged him closer and he took her to a place where there were no rodeos and no bulls.

A SOFT BREEZE buffeting his shoulder woke Johnny. He rolled his head on the pillow and discovered the air was Shannon's breath against the side of his neck.

This afternoon in her bed proved that the first time he'd made love with her at the Hacienda Motel hadn't been a fluke. He'd lost himself so completely in her that not once during the experience had he thought about her as his sister's best friend or the little girl he'd looked out for at the farm.

He studied her face in the fading sunlight. The dark circles beneath her eyes concerned him. He'd been surprised that she'd admitted to having nightmares and he felt a powerful urge to protect her from those demons. He'd fought all kinds of battles for his brothers and sister—battles with teachers, coaches, employers, friends and irate fathers, but he'd never had to fight an enemy he couldn't see.

The fact that Shannon intended to compete in Tucson scared the hell out of him. Along with that fear, his heart ached for the pain she'd kept locked inside her all these years as a result of her mother's abandonment. Johnny's sister had been fortunate to have a grandmother to fill the role of mother when Aimee Cash had come and gone in their lives, but Shannon had had no one.

Until her confession, he hadn't given a whole lot of thought to his own father's abandonment. He suspected the driving need behind his insistence on taking care of others was a direct result of wanting that same attention for himself from his biological father. As he grew older, assuming the role of father toward his siblings came naturally, but he admitted there were times through the years when he'd just wanted to be a brother and not have to worry about anyone but himself.

If Shannon was determined to go after a national title there was nothing he or anyone else could do to stop her, but if she didn't find a way to conquer her fear, the title would remain out of reach and she'd put herself at greater risk each time she competed. His chest tightened at the thought of anything happening to her. He couldn't pinpoint the exact moment, place or time when concern over her getting hurt evolved into feelings far deeper and richer. If the fear he felt for her wasn't rooted in love, then he didn't know what love was. He wanted to confess his feelings, but how could he when he finally understood what was pushing her to compete?

Maybe he couldn't stop her from competing against Rodriguez in Tucson, but he refused to stand by and watch her get hurt again. The only way he knew how to keep her safe was to help her conquer her fear of bulls.

Chapter Twelve

Shannon awoke from a deep sleep to the *yip, yip, yip* sounds of the Gila woodpecker outside her bedroom window. She didn't need to open her eyes to know she was alone in the bed. She breathed in Johnny's scent, which lingered on the sheets, then stretched her arms above her head. She was sore in places that had never been sore from all her years of riding bulls.

She rolled onto her side and pressed her face into Johnny's pillow. She didn't want to leave the bed. After the first round of lovemaking they'd eaten dinner and returned to her room, waking twice during the night to make love. At four in the morning, they'd shared a bowl of cereal in bed and then had fallen asleep in each other's arms. And amazingly her sleep had been free of nightmares.

Although neither of them had spoken the words out loud, Shannon had repeated "I love you" over and over in her head while they'd kissed. Falling in love with Johnny hadn't surprised her one tiny bit—he'd been a part of her life for so long that it only made sense that the affection she'd held for him through the years had evolved into a richer and deeper emotion.

What had caught her by surprise was her desperate

desire to please him. The realization scared her sense-
less and prevented her from confessing her love. Admit-
ting her true feelings would give Johnny too much power
over her. Then if he asked her not to compete in Tucson,
she'd cave in and withdraw from the event.

The Gila woodpecker continued to serenade her, so
she gave up on sleep. The first step of the day was the
most painful, even after she stretched her calf muscle.
Today was no different as she limped across the room
and stood in front of the window overlooking the barn
and corral.

Johnny was saddling Bear in the round pen. The sight
of him calmed her until she glanced at the mechanical
bull behind the barn, and then she shuddered. Come January she'd face C.J. in their final ride-off and her fears
would have to take a backseat to beating the cowboy and
winning the title.

When Johnny attempted to place the saddle on Bear,
the horse reared. Johnny stood his ground—cowboy and
horse locked in a battle of wills.

You'll never win this one, Bear.

Johnny set the saddle down, pulled a horse treat from
his pocket and placed it on the saddle before moving
away. Bear sniffed the leather seat, ate the treat and
stomped the saddle with his front hoof before bolting
across the pen.

Shannon laughed and right then Johnny glanced toward the house and his gaze connected with hers. Her
heart sighed when he touched his finger to the brim of
his hat and dipped his head.

She hurried into the bathroom to shower and dress for
the day. Afterward she packed a picnic lunch of crack-

ers and cheese. She added a bottle of wine she found in the pantry, napkins, a knife, a wine opener and bottles of water, then set the cooler by the front door while she fetched a quilt from the linen closet upstairs. She called for Hank and they left the house.

"Nice boots," Johnny said when she stopped at the corral.

"Thanks." She was secretly pleased he liked her fancy black Ariat boots with sapphire stitching, beaded embroidery and a silk-screen design over the toe of the boot.

"Rock'n'roll sass with a little cowgirl class."

Feeling shy after spending the night naked in his arms, she said, "These are my date-night boots."

"Are you going on a date?"

"Depends."

"On...?"

"Whether or not you'd care to join me for a picnic."

He glanced at his watch. "At ten o'clock in the morning?"

She nodded to the horse. "It doesn't look like you're making much progress with Bear. Maybe you both need a break."

"Insulting the horse trainer won't earn you any points."

"C'mon, Johnny. It's a beautiful day." The temperature had already reached sixty-five and the sun shone bright in a cloudless sky. "Don't make me take off my date-night boots."

"Is this a horseback-ride picnic or a truck-tailgate picnic?"

"Tailgate. Hank would like to join us."

Johnny rubbed the hound's ears. "If it's all right with

you, we'll picnic out at the windmill. I need to replace one of the vanes."

"Sure."

"Take my truck," he said. "The keys are on the kitchen table."

While Johnny put Bear's saddle in the barn, Shannon went to the cabin and found the keys resting next to an envelope from a bank. The word *Urgent* had been stamped on the front. Was it a credit card bill that Johnny hadn't paid, or a notice pertaining to the pecan farm?

It's none of your business.

Maybe not, but after making love last night weren't they—

A couple?

She'd fallen in love with Johnny but that didn't mean he felt the same way about her. Doubts crowded her thoughts. What if he'd made love to her out of pity? Had he been her consolation prize after an embarrassing afternoon at the rodeo? The cabin door opened and Johnny caught her red-handed holding the envelope.

Too late to act as if she'd picked it up by accident, she asked, "Is everything all right at the farm?"

"The farm's fine." He took the envelope from her and placed it on the kitchen counter. "Let's get going. Later this afternoon I need to move the herd and work with Bear again."

"We can picnic another time, if you're too busy."

He grasped her face and pressed his mouth against hers. "Does that feel like a man wanting an excuse not to spend time with a beautiful woman?"

"Not really."

"I must be losing my touch." This time when his lips found her, he thrust his tongue inside her mouth.

The kiss was hot, wet and a little wild. When they came up for air, she said, "I'm convinced."

Johnny's truck had a bench seat, and when she got in on the driver's side and attempted to scoot across the seat, he said, "Stay right where you are."

He lowered the tailgate, then lifted Hank into the bed before hopping behind the wheel. They drove in silence and Shannon's skin shivered each time Johnny's thigh nudged hers when the truck hit a rut in the road.

Once they arrived at the windmill, Johnny helped Hank to the ground and the dog trotted off to explore, while Shannon spread the blanket in the truck bed and rummaged through the cooler.

"In Hank's canine youth he'd turn a stray cow toward the herd, then leap back into Roger's moving pickup," Johnny said.

"Dad claims Hank is the best cow dog he's ever owned."

"Then you came home from the hospital and turned Hank into a big baby."

Shannon laughed.

"While you set out the food I'll take care of this." Johnny removed the new vane he'd ordered three weeks ago, grabbed his tools and climbed the thirty-foot tower of the antique 1935 Aermotor windmill. He had noticed the damaged vane after a storm had blown through the area and the best he could figure was that a gust of wind had slammed a piece of heavy debris into the vane, denting the metal. He removed the damaged vane and bolted the new one to the tailbone section. After he climbed down, he examined the pump.

It worried him how quickly he'd agreed to the picnic with Shannon, and then when they'd gotten in his truck he'd wanted her sitting next to him, bodies touching. It hadn't been like this with Charlene, not even in the beginning during their first few dates. He was amazed that he'd spent an entire night in Shannon's bed and not once during that time had he thought about their age difference. Or the upcoming rodeo in Tucson. Or training Bear to accept a saddle. He hadn't even remembered the bank statement sitting in the foreman's cabin.

Shannon had consumed his thoughts and his heart the entire time he'd been in bed with her. At dawn, he'd dressed and left the house, fearing if she opened her eyes, he'd fall captive to her pleading look and dive between the sheets with her again. As it was, he could barely concentrate on chores without recalling her sweet scent and how soft her feet had felt when they'd glided up his calf and touched his…

He shook his head to clear his mind of lusty thoughts then tightened the pump rod and checked the drive gear to make sure it didn't stick. When he joined Shannon on the tailgate, he stared at the crackers and cheese and bottle of wine. "Is that all there is to eat?"

"Sorry, there was no lunch meat in the fridge." She handed him the opener for the bottle.

Johnny wasn't a big wine drinker, but he appreciated Shannon's effort to make the picnic special. She held out plastic cups and he filled them.

"A toast," she said. "To—"

"To you." He tapped the edge of his cup against hers,

then nuzzled her neck. When he kissed the skin near her ear, she made a purring sound that drove him crazy.

She pulled back first, her mouth turning up at the corners in a shy smile. He liked this softer side to the tough lady bull rider. "Do you think your father's enjoying the cruise?"

"I hope so. I've noticed he's mellowed since Thanksgiving. I'm sure Fiona has a lot to do with that."

"He's been tough on you, hasn't he?"

"Let's not talk about my father. Instead, can I ask you a question?"

The hairs on the back of his neck vibrated. Nothing good came out of a conversation that started with "Can I ask you a question?" "Sure."

"I know our age difference bothers you."

"It doesn't bother me as much anymore." What worried him now was falling hard for a woman who might be here one day and gone the next. He wasn't ready to admit his feelings for Shannon—not until he knew for certain he could stand by her all the way to the end—wherever that took them. He grasped her hand and squeezed. "You make me feel things I've never felt before." He brought her hand to his mouth and kissed her knuckles. "You challenge me at every turn but when you're in my arms you feel like you're meant to be there." Whether Shannon rode in Tucson or not wouldn't change that fact.

She lifted her face to him and he kissed her, then worked the buttons on her blouse loose before slipping his hand inside and caressing her breast. Her breath grew ragged as he toyed with her belt buckle, but that's as far as he got when his cell phone went off.

He fished the phone from his back pocket with an

apologetic glance at Shannon. "Hey, P.T. It's Johnny. Thanks for returning my call."

P. T. Lewis was the owner of Five Star Ranch, a sanctuary for retired rodeo stock. Shannon had practiced many times on P.T.'s bulls over the past few years. She wondered why Johnny had reached out to the man.

"You bet." Johnny checked his watch. "We can be out there within the hour. Thanks, P.T."

"What was that all about?" Shannon asked.

"P.T. agreed to let you practice on his bulls. We can visit the ranch anytime we want as long as we call ahead."

"What do you mean *we?*"

Johnny's blue eyes warmed. "You and me." He took her hand and threaded his fingers through hers. "I'm going to do everything in my power to make sure you're ready to compete in January."

She sucked in a quick breath. "I thought you didn't want me to rodeo."

"I don't. But I also know nothing's going to stop you, and if you're determined to ride in three weeks, I want to make sure you're prepared."

She flung her arms around his neck. "I knew you wouldn't let me down."

"Looks like we'll have to put our picnic on hold." He kissed her, then dumped the wine from his cup over the side of the truck.

"We'll eat later," she said, shoving the food into the cooler. Within a minute they had everything packed. She whistled for Hank and the dog came running. Johnny lifted him into the truck bed then secured the tailgate and they drove back to the house, Shannon feeling more confident by the second that with Johnny's help she'd be ready to compete in Tucson.

As soon as Johnny parked next to the round pen at Five Star Ranch, the front door of the hacienda-style house opened and P. T. Lewis stepped outside.

"You don't look too bad for a gal who got in a bull wreck a couple of months ago." The white-haired rancher's eyes twinkled as his gaze traveled over Shannon's body.

"Thanks, P.T. I'm almost good as new," she said.

"Heard you took Roger's place as foreman of the Triple D." P.T. shook hands with Johnny.

"I'm fortunate to be working for Clive. He's a good man."

"Nobody trains better cutting horses than Clive." P.T. motioned to the corral and began walking. "I picked up a rodeo bull a few weeks ago from a ranch in New Mexico." He glanced at Shannon. "Don't know if you've ever ridden him."

"What's his name?" she asked.

"Pistol Pete."

"Doesn't sound familiar," she said. They stopped at the corral.

Johnny thought the solid black bull looked like a doofus with his horns sawed off unevenly.

"He bucks three times then spins." P.T. shook his head. "He became too predictable so they retired him."

Johnny considered the bull's body. He looked to be in good shape. "How old is he?"

"Six. He's got a lot of gas left in him."

Shannon shielded her eyes from the sun. "Why is he being kept by himself in the pen behind the barn?"

"He's aggressive with the other bulls. The old-timers don't want anything to do with him."

"What happened to Curly?" she asked.

P.T. nodded to the open space on the other side of the barn. "He's lounging in the shade."

"You don't keep him penned up anymore?" Shannon asked.

"You remember Lauren, don't you? Clint's daughter?"

"Sure."

"She's away at college now, but she's claimed Curly as her personal pet. That dang bull won't leave the ranch yard now."

Johnny found that incredible. "He never wanders off?"

"Not anymore. He even naps by the front door."

"Does Curly still buck?" Shannon's teeth nibbled her lower lip and Johnny wondered if she was having second thoughts about riding. Maybe Pistol Pete was more than she could handle right now.

"Sure Curly bucks. Want to take a run at him instead of Pistol Pete?"

"Why not. For old time's sake."

"Get your gear on. I'll go fetch him."

As soon as P.T. walked out of earshot, Johnny said, "If you don't feel ready, that's okay. We can come back tomorrow."

"I have to do this." She put on her Kevlar vest and protective headgear.

P.T. loaded Curly into a makeshift chute and Johnny remained inside the pen, ready to open the gate when she signaled.

He waited for her to climb onto Curly's back but she didn't budge from the top rail. He couldn't get a good look at her eyes through the wire face mask but he noticed that she'd forgotten to put on her riding glove.

She's nervous.

When P.T. glanced his way, Johnny gave a nod, signaling that he was aware of Shannon's hesitation.

"If you two don't mind," P.T. said, "I've got business calls to make. I'll be in the house if you need me."

As soon as the rancher walked off, Shannon expelled a loud breath.

"You okay?" Johnny asked.

"Nerves I guess."

He wanted to mention the riding glove but Shannon would figure that out soon enough. Right now she had to overcome her fear of climbing onto Curly's back.

She eased onto the bull's back and wiggled into position. Johnny handed her the end of the bull rope and Shannon cursed. "Why didn't you tell me I'd forgotten to put on my glove?" She hopped off and rummaged through her gear bag. With her glove on she climbed the rails and dropped onto Curly's back. Not until she reached for the rope again did she realize what she'd done. She cracked a smile. "Maybe the trick is staying pissed off."

"Maybe."

She took her time securing her grip. He wanted to tell her that second-guessing the wrap would only whittle away at her confidence, but he remained silent, giving her room to work through her anxiety. Satisfied with her grip, she braced herself and said, "Ready."

He opened the gate and Curly jumped out. His bucks were solid but he had no speed or energy, which allowed

Shannon to make adjustments with her body and test the strength in her leg.

He counted the seconds off in his head and was pleased when eight came and went and Shannon continued to ride, working on her rhythm. After a few more seconds he saw her gaze shift to the ground and he knew she was looking for an opening to dismount. When Curly came out of his spin, she released the rope and pushed off with her left leg. She landed too close to Curly, but the bull trotted off and proved no threat. Shannon got to her feet, took one step and stumbled.

He lurched forward and grasped her shoulders. "What's wrong?"

"Leg cramp."

Johnny wanted to believe Shannon's leg would get better with time but he had serious doubts the tendon would ever be a hundred percent again.

She limped back to the chute.

After coaxing Curly into the space, he waited for Shannon to give him the signal. It wasn't until the fifth go-round that she raised her hand for help getting off the ground.

"I think we're done." He tugged her to her feet.

"I'll tell you when I've had enough."

He stepped in front of her when she attempted to walk back to the chute. "Look, Shannon. There's no sense pushing yourself too hard today—not if you want to return tomorrow and practice."

Her shoulders sagged. "You're right." She piled her gear inside the bag and he tossed it into the truck bed.

"I'll take Curly back to his spot next to the barn, then run up to the house and tell P.T. we're leaving."

"Johnny." Tears shimmered in her eyes.

Damn it, she'd pushed herself too hard. He should have stopped her after she'd ridden Curly twice. "What?"

"Thank you for helping me. I couldn't have done it without you."

He squeezed her hand. "Hang tight. I'll get you home so you can ice your leg."

THE TRIP TO Five Star Ranch set up a pattern for the next several days. Johnny did ranch chores early in the morning, and then he and Shannon made the drive to P.T.'s to practice in the afternoon, and later at night he helped her work on the mechanical bull back at the Triple D. Dead tired, he crammed in an hour training Bear before bed. He needed to make more time for the horse but Shannon was his first priority.

The day of reckoning had arrived—Clive was due home tomorrow and although Johnny had gotten Bear to accept a saddle, the horse still wouldn't allow Johnny to ride him. Intending to fix that now, he saddled the gelding and put him in the corral.

"Stay calm, big guy." Johnny tied the reins to the rail and slung a leg over the horse. As soon as his butt hit the leather, Bear reared and Johnny went flying.

"Damn it, Bear." He fetched his hat and jammed it on his head. Once the horse relaxed, he made another attempt to sit in the saddle and landed in the dirt again.

"You're a good match for him."

Johnny glanced across the pen where Shannon watched.

"How so?" he asked, wincing when a sharp pain shot through his butt muscle.

"You're both stubborn." She motioned to the bucking machine. "Got a minute? I could use your advice."

"Sure." He untied Bear, then patted his rump. "We're not finished, hotshot. I'll be back.

"What's wrong?" he asked when he caught up with Shannon.

"I'm ready to admit that my leg won't be healed by the time I compete in Tucson and dismounting the traditional way isn't going to get the job done."

He'd suggested she needed to learn a different dismount but Shannon had been convinced with more practice she could master the old way. That she finally admitted defeat didn't reassure Johnny in the least.

"Show me your regular dismount," he said.

Shannon hopped on the mechanical bull and rode until she found an opening, then pushed off but didn't land far enough away. If she'd been on a real bull she would have fallen under its belly and gotten stomped. A lot of good it would do for her to make it to eight and win the title only to end up trampled.

"You're going to have to dismount on the right side." He hopped on the bull. "Chris Cummings did this two years ago in Phoenix when he rode with a busted left leg." Cummings was a top-ten bull rider on the circuit.

Shannon stood by the controls, waiting for Johnny to give her the signal to increase the speed.

"Once the buzzer sounds watch for the bull to spin left." He nodded at the controls, and Shannon increased the speed. "Cummings leaned back instead of forward and pushed off with his right leg." The machine whipped to the left and Johnny moved into position then launched himself through the air and landed a good four feet away. "Your turn."

Shannon hopped on and found her rhythm. "Lean back," he said. "Ready?"

She nodded.

"One...two...three."

Using her right leg to shove off she flung herself to the side, but her landing was sloppy.

"How did that feel?" he asked.

"Not as uncomfortable as I expected. I think it might work if I keep at it."

A horn honked in the distant and Johnny recognized Clive's truck. "Looks like your father got home a day early," he said.

"Who's that behind him?" Shannon asked.

Johnny noticed the second truck towed a horse trailer and his stomach dropped. "I don't know, but we'll find out soon enough."

Chapter Thirteen

"Hey, Dad," Shannon said when her father stepped from his truck. "We didn't expect you until tomorrow."

"Fiona's niece was in a car accident up in Sedona, so we caught an earlier flight back."

"Is she okay?" Shannon asked.

"She suffered whiplash, but she'll be fine."

A tall, slim man with gray sideburns stepped from the other vehicle and joined the group.

"This is Gary McGovern," Clive said.

Johnny offered his hand. "Johnny Cash. Nice to meet you."

"And you must be the famous Shannon Douglas." Gary tipped his hat. "You've earned quite a reputation in rodeo, young lady."

"Gary's here to see Bear," Clive said, ending talk of Shannon's rodeo successes.

"I'll fetch him from the barn." Johnny made a hasty escape. His gut told him this wasn't going to go well. He stopped outside Bear's stall. "Look, I know you don't like the saddle, but you've got to be on your best behavior." Johnny led the gelding outside and set him free in the round pen, then went back into the barn to fetch the saddle.

"Bear's a stubborn horse," Johnny said, "but if you have patience with him, you won't find a better cow pony."

"Saddle him up," Clive said.

Johnny wished he'd thought to bring a peppermint with him this morning. He carried the saddle across the pen, stopping in front of the horse. "Sorry, buddy. I don't have any treats with me."

He placed the saddle blanket over Bear and released a quiet breath when the horse stood motionless. "That a boy." Slowly he set the saddle on his back. "Easy now." When he was certain Bear wouldn't bolt, he tightened the cinch and walked the gelding across the pen.

"He's a beauty," Gary said.

"Bear loves chasing cattle, but he's got a mind of his own and prefers working without a cowboy on his back," Clive said. "Johnny's been training him." Clive swung his gaze to Johnny. "He'll accept a rider now, won't he?"

Time would tell. Johnny set his foot in the stirrup and froze when Bear's muscles tensed. He counted to three, then swung his right leg over the horse. He had only a second to brace himself before Bear bolted across the pen, stopped on a dime and reared, throwing Johnny on his head.

Busted.

"Doesn't look like Bear's made much progress," Gary said. "I'm sorry, Clive, I can't have an unpredictable horse on my ranch when I've got cowboys coming and going in shifts riding different horses each time."

"Give us another week to work with Bear." Clive shot Johnny a dark look before trailing Gary back to his vehicle.

"Damn you, Bear." Even as Johnny cursed the horse,

he accepted the blame for Bear's disappointing behavior. Once Gary McGovern drove off, Johnny came face-to-face with his boss's wrath.

"You'd better have a damn good reason for Bear not being trained," Clive said. "I asked you to do one thing while I was gone—make sure that horse was ready to sell."

"Dad—"

"You're fired, Johnny."

"Dad!"

Stunned, Johnny stood immobile.

"You can't fire him," Shannon said.

Clive thumped his hat against his thigh. "I gave you a job—" he spoke to Johnny "—and you didn't follow orders."

Johnny felt sick to his stomach. He'd just screwed up the opportunity of a lifetime because he hadn't been able to walk away from Shannon and leave well enough alone. If he needed more proof why he should have resisted his attraction to her, Clive had just given it to him.

"It's not Johnny's fault that Bear isn't ready to sell," Shannon said.

"Then whose fault is it?"

Johnny's boots grew roots in the dirt and he couldn't have moved if he wanted to.

"Mine." She jutted her chin.

Clive glanced between his daughter and Johnny. "What have you got to do with my foreman's responsibilities?"

"Shannon, this is between me and your father," Johnny said.

"No, it's not." She glanced at Johnny, then continued.

"The reason Bear isn't trained yet is because Johnny's been helping me prepare for the rodeo next month."

Clive's mouth dropped open and then he snapped it shut. "I don't know which one of you I'm more disappointed in." He stared at Johnny. "Pack your belongings and leave. I'll put your paycheck in the mail." Clive walked away.

"You're not leaving, Johnny." Shannon ducked between the rails of the pen. "I'll talk to him after he cools off."

He swept a strand of hair from her eyes and wished for both their sakes this hadn't happened, but he'd screwed up. "Don't worry about me. I'll be fine. You make things right with your father." He moved her aside, unsaddled Bear and carried the equipment into the barn.

Shannon followed him. "Please, Johnny, don't go."

Steeling himself against her pleas, he put the saddle away and walked to the foreman's cabin. His boss was a man of his word and Johnny had known the risks when he'd decided to help Shannon train. Once inside the cabin he stuffed his clothes into duffel bags and gathered his toiletries, CDs and his laptop. The rest belonged to Clive—except the beer in the fridge. Johnny took the six-pack of Bud Light. He'd need a drink later when it sunk in that he was unemployed.

He loaded the luggage in the backseat of his truck, then placed the Weber grill—coals and all—in the bed. He sped off, resisting the urge to glance in the rearview mirror—knowing Shannon stood in the driveway, staring after him. It wasn't until he made it to the highway that he remembered the next mortgage payment on the farm was due in two weeks.

JOHNNY HEARD A DOOR slam and went to the bunkhouse window to see who'd shown up at the farm. *Dixie.* Oh, hell. His brothers had called in the cavalry.

Hands on her hips, Dixie squared off with his siblings, who lounged like lazy hound dogs on the front porch. He couldn't hear what she said, but he assumed she was miffed at having to leave her gift shop early during the holiday season. Mack pointed to the bunkhouse and Johnny ducked out of sight. A second later a knock sounded on the door.

"Johnny, let me in. I swear to God if you don't, I'll bust the door down."

It probably wasn't a good thing for a pregnant woman to be upset, so he opened the door and Dixie stepped inside.

"Told you so!" Conway yelled across the yard. "You're Johnny's favorite!"

He shut the door and slid the bolt in place.

"What's this nonsense about locking yourself in the bunkhouse and not letting anyone in?" Before he had a chance to answer, she asked, "Why are you even here? Shouldn't you be at the Triple D?"

"I got fired today."

"Fired? Clive wouldn't fire you."

"He would and he did." Johnny took a beer from the fridge and dropped onto the sofa.

"What happened?" Dixie sat on the coffee table in front of him.

"I don't want to talk about it."

"Does Shannon have anything to do with you getting fired?"

He gaped at his sister. Had Shannon confided in Dixie about their relationship?

"Did you sleep with her?"

He nodded. "But that has nothing to do with why I was fired." He gulped his beer. "I didn't get a horse trained in time to sell to a buyer and Clive was counting on making that sale."

"Why didn't you train the horse?"

"Because I was too busy helping Shannon get over her fear of riding again."

Dixie frowned. "She never told me she was afraid of riding bulls."

"She's had nightmares since her wreck on Heat Miser, then she scratched at the Chula Vista rodeo and her confidence took a nosedive."

"How were you helping her?"

"We've been spending a lot of time working on the mechanical bull and then we started going to P. T. Lewis's place so she could practice on Curly." He stared at the ground. "I don't know if it's enough, Dixie."

"What do you mean 'enough'?"

"Shannon's scared. The worst thing she can do is ride a bull if she has doubts in her mind. She needs to accept that her bull riding days are over." He got up from the couch and stared out the window overlooking the orchard.

"Shannon's the most courageous woman I know. The only way she wouldn't ride in Tucson is if she physically couldn't get on the bull."

"Well, it's out of my hands now."

"Does Shannon know why her father fired you?"

"She was there. She tried to intervene, but that upset Clive even more, so I got the heck out of there."

"Are you in love with Shannon, Johnny?"

He faced his sister. He could deny it all he wanted but it wouldn't change the truth. "Yes, I am."

"Then this will all work out. Give Clive time to get over being mad and he'll—"

"I don't care whether or not Clive offers me my job back." He waved a hand in the air as if swatting at a fly. "There's no future for me and Shannon if she's determined to continue competing."

"You're going to abandon her when she needs you most?"

"I can't be with a woman who puts herself in harm's way, knowing she isn't prepared and that she could get badly injured or even killed."

"Have you told her that you love her?"

He felt his neck grow warm. "Not in so many words."

"It wasn't very long ago," Dixie said, "you pointed out to me that when you love someone, you love all of them—the good and the bad."

"This is different. Gavin had to obey military orders—he didn't have a choice when he was deployed to Afghanistan. Shannon has a choice. She doesn't have to ride in Tucson."

"But, Johnny, her whole life has been dedicated to chasing this title. If you love her, then you'll be by her side no matter what the outcome."

He was the eldest. He was the one who doled out advice in their family and he didn't like having to listen to his sister even if what she said made sense. He'd figure out the mess between him and Shannon later.

Time to address another issue—one that directly involved Dixie. "Now that I lost my job at the Triple D, we've got a problem with the farm." He removed the bank statement from his pocket and handed it to her.

"I don't understand," she said. "Does this mean I might lose the house?"

"And the orchards, too."

"How did this happen?"

Johnny did his best to condense two years' worth of information on rising interest rates and agricultural companies downsizing.

"And you didn't think to share any of this with me?" Dixie shook the envelope in his face. "I should have never let you talk me into allowing the bank to send you the mortgage statements on the farm."

"C'mon, Dix. You were too young to handle that kind of financial responsibility after Grandma died."

He wasn't used to disappointing others and he tried to defend himself. "And you were in no shape to discuss the farm a year ago when you were pregnant. Then you and Gavin bought the gift shop in Yuma and soon after you had a miscarriage. Then it was touch and go on whether you and Gavin would stay together. When was I supposed to tell you that the farm was in trouble?"

"I'm sorry," she said. "I didn't mean to jump down your throat. But you could have mentioned the situation after Gavin and I married."

"By then I thought I'd solved the problem. I found a company to harvest this year's crop, and I knew I could pay the mortgage once I began working at the Triple D."

"But this letter—" she rattled the paper in the air "—says you've missed three mortgage payments."

"That happened right after Grandma died and the agricultural company didn't renew their lease with the farm. It took a few months to sign on with another company."

"I wish you would have told me, Johnny. I could have pitched in money to make up the missed payments."

If he could go back and change the way he'd handled the farm business, he would.

"I don't understand why all of a sudden the bank is calling in the loan now," she said.

"It's because we haven't leased out the farm yet."

"We don't have to, do we? Can't we take over the pecan production?"

"*We* meaning who, Dixie? You're too busy with the gift shop. Gavin works full-time for the city of Yuma, and the rest of us have never shown much interest in harvesting pecans once Grandpa died."

"I can sympathize with the tight spot you were in after Grandma passed away, but this wasn't your decision to make alone."

His sister might as well have kicked his legs out from under him. "I've been taking care of this family for a long time. When no one else gave a crap about the farm, I made phone calls and begged agricultural companies to lease the orchards. I've busted my ass to hang on to this property because I promised Grandpa on his deathbed I wouldn't lose the farm."

"Johnny, I love you. You're the best big brother a girl could ever want. But right now I'm angry—angry because you want to protect me from bad news." Dixie rubbed her brow. "You've done an amazing job keeping this family together after Grandpa and Grandma died, but we're all adults now. You can stop being our father and just be our brother."

"What do you think we should do about the farm?"

Dixie stuck her head out the door and whistled. "Family meeting!"

His brothers filed into the bunkhouse and sat at the picnic table, and then his sister spoke. "Johnny has something to tell us."

No sense beating around the bush. "The farm's in financial trouble."

"What do you mean?" Conway asked.

"Give him a chance to explain," Dixie said.

He condensed the past few years into a few sentences, then ended his spiel with "I don't have enough money left in my savings to pay off the bank and now that I no longer work for the Triple D I won't be able to make the monthly mortgage."

"Damn it, Johnny." Conway banged his fist on the table. "You should have come to us sooner for help."

Feeling cornered, he fought back. "And what would you have done? What would any of you have done?" He spread his arms wide. "You're all wrapped up in your own lives, just like always. No one has shown any interest in growing pecans for years. Every one of you assumed I'd take care of things." He blew out a breath and got a hold of his temper. "I was handling the mortgage payments just fine until Clive fired me."

"Why'd he fire you?" Mack asked the question.

"Never mind that," Dixie said. "Let's hear ideas on how we're going to save the farm."

"Maybe we don't save it," Buck said. "Maybe we sell the orchards and Dixie keeps the house and the barn."

"I promised Grandpa Ely that the pecan trees would remain in the family," Johnny said. "I realize that none of us is gung ho on working the land—"

"Speak for yourself," Conway said. "Did you ever ask any of us if we wanted to get involved in managing the farm?"

"No, but no one was stopping you from speaking up."

"Enough!" Dixie sliced her hand through the air and her brothers quit grumbling. "Johnny did what he thought was best for all of us at the time. From now on, we're in this together. The success of the farm shouldn't rest on one person's shoulders."

Conway wasn't done picking a fight with Johnny. "If you'd told us about the missed mortgage payments after Grandma died we could have helped."

"Help how?" Johnny asked. "You weren't making any money on the rodeo circuit." He pointed at his brothers. "And the rest of you were more interested in chasing women than working an extra job to pay off debts."

"It's different now." Conway faced his siblings. "I say we vote Johnny out of head of household."

"For God's sake, Conway," Dixie said. "This isn't an episode of *Big Brother*."

"I'm serious." Conway stared Johnny in the eye. "I'll take over the farm."

A chorus of "What?" echoed through the room.

"I'll manage the farm," Conway said. "I know Grandpa and Grandma left the place to Dixie, but she's married, expecting a baby and running her own business." Conway addressed each brother. "Mack, you're busy with your band and babysitting wannabe cowboys at the dude ranch. Will, you're picking up more construction work with Ben Wallace's company. Buck, you're thinking about buying into Troy Winters's car-repair business and Porter—" Conway shook his head. "Hell if anyone knows what you're gonna do with your life." Conway faced Johnny. "I'm the logical choice to take over the farm. I can cut back on rodeo and—"

"You don't know a thing about agricultural companies and what I've had to deal with the past several years."

"Then I'll learn just like you did." Conway's brown eyes pleaded with Johnny and it was then he realized his brother was dead serious. Why the brother who was the biggest flirt with women wanted to tie himself down to a pecan orchard was beyond Johnny.

"Let's put it to a vote," Dixie said. "All in favor of Conway running the farm raise your hands."

Dixie, Mack, Buck, Will and Porter all raised their hands. The majority had spoken. Who was Johnny to stand in his brother's way?

"Good. That's settled. In the meantime, we need to come up with the cash to pay off the bank," Dixie said. "I'm broke. Everything Gavin and I have is invested in the gift shop."

The rest of the Cash brothers volunteered part of their savings to cover the past-due bill from the bank and each of them agreed to contribute toward the monthly mortgage until Conway came up with a plan for the farm.

Dixie and his brothers filed out of the bunkhouse, but Conway stopped at the door. "Johnny."

"What?"

"You've done a lot for all of us through the years. I won't disappoint you."

He was ashamed that he'd come down so hard on Conway. "I know you won't. And I'll do what I can to help you."

JOHNNY WIPED HIS shirtsleeve across his brow and watched Conway drive the tractor out of the barn. He and his brother had spent the morning tuning up the piece of equipment to see if they could get another year's harvest out of the fifteen-year-old machine before they were forced to buy a new one.

His cell phone went off and he checked the number—Porter. His younger brother had left a couple of hours ago to compete in the Growler rodeo. "What's wrong, Porter? Did you get hurt?"

"The rodeo hasn't even started."

Johnny checked his watch—ten-thirty. He'd been up since 5:00 a.m. He'd thought more time had passed.

"You'll never believe who's here."

A cold chill raced down Johnny's spine.

"Shannon."

"Is Rodriguez there, too?" Johnny asked.

"Haven't seen him or the Dynasty Boots tent."

Shannon had gone rogue.

"But that's not the only thing strange," Porter said.

"What do you mean?"

"I was walking past the women's restroom as Shannon stepped out, and when she saw me, she did an about-face and went back into the bathroom."

"Are you sure it was Shannon?"

"Positive. She walked with a limp."

What the hell was she doing at the rodeo?

"One more thing."

"What?"

"When I went to sign in, I asked to look at the roster of bull riders. She signed in as Shane Douglas."

Damn it. "When does she ride?"

"One-thirty."

"Thanks." Johnny disconnected the call. He didn't wait to tell Conway he was leaving the farm. He ran to the bunkhouse, grabbed his truck keys and hat, then took off. If he pushed the speed limit, he'd arrive in Growler by one. He forced his thoughts to remain on the road and not drift to Shannon, because if he pictured her competing, he'd go crazy.

He hadn't seen her since Clive had fired him. Christmas had come and gone and no phone call. No text. Nothing. Since he'd spent time helping her and had lost his job because of it, he'd at least expected her to check in on him, but she hadn't.

Now you know why she never phoned. Shannon knew he'd have tried to talk her out of competing today.

Shannon wasn't ready to ride. She was still grappling with her fear and she hadn't perfected her dismount off the right side of the bucking machine. Hell, he didn't even know if she'd practiced on the mechanical bull since he'd been fired. If she was determined to ride in Tucson, why would she risk injury in a two-bit local rodeo?

By the time Johnny arrived at the outdoor rodeo grounds, his heart was hammering inside his chest. He parked in the far corner of the lot and jogged through the maze of vehicles to the event center entrance. He went straight to the cowboy ready area. Shannon was nowhere. Maybe Porter had been mistaken. Then he saw her blue gear bag beneath a stool.

"She's in there." Porter nodded to the restroom. "I've been hanging out here since I called you. She's tried twice to leave the bathroom but when she sees me she runs back inside."

"Bet she's pissed at you," Johnny said.

"What are you going to do?"

"Keep her from getting hurt today." Johnny made his way to the sign-in table and spoke with the rodeo secretary. He explained that *Shane Douglas* would be withdrawing from the bull riding event due to flu-like symptoms.

The secretary objected, insisting *Shane* needed to sign himself out, but Johnny convinced her to scratch him off the list after telling her that he was out in the parking lot puking.

When Johnny returned to the chutes, Porter asked, "What did you do?"

"Signed her out."

His brother whistled between his teeth. "She isn't going to like that."

If Shannon wanted to compete in Tucson she couldn't risk an injury today. Besides, if she was hell-bent on winning a title, then she should wait until she was a hundred percent healthy.

"I don't want to be here when she finds out what you did." Porter patted Johnny on the shoulder and joined his competitors hanging out by the horses.

"Ladies and gentlemen, welcome to the..."

Johnny's ears shut out the announcer as he waited in front of the ladies' restroom. When Shannon limped out and saw him, the blood drained from her face. She glanced to her right and then to her left, as if searching for an escape. When she realized there was nowhere to run she walked up to him.

"What are you doing here?" she asked.

"Protecting you."

"From what?"

"You're not ready to ride."

"The hell I'm not."

"You limped all the way over here." He lowered his voice. "Have you practiced dismounting off the right side?"

"All week."

"What about on a real bull out at P.T.'s place?"

She straightened her shoulders. "I don't need you to fight my battles and—"

"But I was good enough for you when I lost my job helping you, right?" He hadn't meant to use that against her, but her stubbornness tested his patience.

"I'm sorry my father fired you, but I'm tired of people telling me what I should and shouldn't do. I'm not the same little girl who played with your sister at the farm. I'm a grown woman who knows my own limitations. If I say I'm ready to ride, then I'm ready to ride. Now get out of my way."

"I'm sorry, Shannon, but I made sure your name was removed from the bull riding event."

She gasped.

"I told them *Shane* had the flu."

Her eyes glistened with tears. "How could you? You were the one person I thought I could count on supporting me." She pushed him aside, grabbed her equipment bag and marched off.

Johnny was tempted to go after her and make sure she got home safe, but he worried she'd run him off the road. She'd probably never speak to him again, but at least she was safe.

For today anyway.

Chapter Fourteen

Shannon was spitting mad. How dare Johnny interfere with her bull ride? Porter must have tipped him off when he'd seen her try to leave the bathroom at the rodeo. Just because she and Johnny had slept together didn't mean he had a say in her rodeo career.

Miles of clay-colored dirt and scrubby cactus whizzed by the truck as she sped down the highway. After a while her anger fizzled to a rolling boil and she admitted— reluctantly—that she was relieved she hadn't ridden this afternoon. She'd gone to the rodeo because she needed reassurance that she could successfully dismount before she competed in Tucson next weekend. Stick of Dynamite was a twenty-three-point bull and a mean one at that. She doubted she'd have made the buzzer.

And she might have been injured again.

Had Johnny saved her from making a grave mistake?

Whether he had or hadn't didn't matter. What hurt the most was that after all the time they'd spent together he didn't view her as a strong mature woman capable of handling herself. When he looked at her, he saw his little sister's childhood friend whom he felt compelled to protect.

Two hours later Shannon pulled up to the house and noticed her father's truck in the driveway. She left her gear bag in the backseat and went to search for him in the barn. She found him in the supply room filling the grain bins.

"You're back early." His gaze roamed over her body. "You okay?"

"I didn't ride."

The frown lines marring her father's brow disappeared. "How come?"

"Johnny Cash withdrew me from the event."

His eyes widened then narrowed. "What's going on between you and Johnny?"

"Do you have time to talk?"

"Sure." He scooped grain into a feed bucket and placed the lid over the barrel. Shannon followed him out to the round pen where he set the bucket inside the corral for Bear.

Before she discussed her own problems, she asked, "How's Fiona's niece?"

"She's home from the hospital."

"Are you and Fiona planning any more trips together?" she asked.

"You going to keep changing the subject or get to what's on your mind?"

"You shouldn't have fired Johnny."

"He didn't do what I asked him to do, Shannon."

"Johnny's been loyal to you all these years and it's only because he was looking out for me that he didn't have enough time to train Bear before you returned from the cruise."

"Johnny knows I don't approve of you riding bulls."

Shannon released a quiet sigh. "Everybody knows you want me to quit rodeo."

"When you were little and mutton bustin' with your brothers, I was proud of you for beating out all the boys."

"I was grand champion three times," she said.

"Then in high school, I was surprised you insisted on riding bulls but they were smaller and not as aggressive, so I didn't make a fuss."

He shook his head. "When you joined the circuit instead of going to college, I realized I didn't know a damned thing about raising a daughter."

"Am I that much of a disappointment?"

"You're not a disappointment, daughter." He kicked a clump of dirt with the toe of his boot. "I feel as if I failed you. You were born a girl and I raised you like a boy. If I could go back in time, I'd do things differently."

"Like how?"

"Well, for one I would have bought you that Barbie for Christmas instead of the Lego set I got your brothers. And I wouldn't have insisted you wear Luke's hand-me-down cowboy boots when you wanted those pink sparkly shoes at Walmart."

"I did plenty of girl things growing up with Dixie at her farm."

"I should have tracked your mother down and made her keep in touch with you."

"Do you honestly believe your parenting technique is the reason I'm riding bulls?"

"You said yourself that you want to win a title because I've got one and so have your brothers."

"That's true. I do want that title. I've come too far now to quit. And I'm not only riding for myself, I'm riding for all the young girls who dream of riding bulls one day."

Her father's eyes shimmered as he stared at her. "What if you don't win the title?" he whispered.

"Then there's always next year."

"If you win the title, then what?"

"I'll cross that road when I come to it." Her entire life had been devoted to rodeo and she had no idea what she'd do with herself when she retired from the sport.

"Nothing I say will stop you from riding in Tucson?"

"No."

Her father turned away, but Shannon clutched his arm. "There is one thing I need you to do for me, Dad."

"What?"

"Give Johnny his job back."

"We've been over this before, Shannon, and—"

"I love him, Dad." She swallowed hard. "He's everything I've dreamed of in a man."

"Then why aren't you two together?"

"I can't be with Johnny, because he won't let me fight my own battles."

Her father shook his head. "You sure don't know the male mind, do you?"

"What do you mean?"

"When a man loves a woman, he'll do everything in his power to keep her safe even if it means losing her."

Shannon watched her father walk off feeling as if she were the one who'd betrayed Johnny, when all along he'd been the one who hadn't understood her.

"LADIES AND GENTLEMEN, welcome to La Fiesta De Los Vaqueros Rodeo this fine Friday afternoon in Tucson!"

Shannon paced in front of the chutes. She and C.J. would kick off the rodeo with their bull rides.

"Shannon Douglas and C. J. Rodriguez have been traveling the country, promoting women's roughstock events." Applause rippled through the stands. "The couple is sponsored by Dynasty Boots and they'll be competing in a best-of-three ride-off this weekend."

She tugged on her riding glove, scaled the chute and waved to the crowd.

C.J. joined her and hammed it up for the cameras. "You ready, Douglas?"

"Sure am."

Keeping his smile in place he whispered, "Heard you scratched in Chula Vista."

"I got sick with the flu."

They dropped down from the chute out of view of the cameras. "Look," C.J. said. "I know how much you want this win but if you're not ready to compete, then don't be a fool and ride. We'll say your leg isn't a hundred percent. People will believe that after your wreck on Heat Miser."

"I'm not going to let you walk away with an easy win."

"If you know I'll win, why risk your neck?" he asked. C.J. took a step but she snagged his shirtsleeve.

"Just for the record…you're not going to win." Shannon focused on the bull the rodeo workers loaded into the chute. Mr. Shorty was a small bull but quick. Bless his heart, he stood docile and calm as the cowboys fished the rope beneath his girth. Mr. Shorty had been on the circuit five years and knew what would happen when the gate opened. Shannon put on her face mask, climbed the rails and straddled his back.

"Better watch out, Douglas." C.J. appeared at her side. "That bull's gonna—"

"Up to your old tricks, Rodriguez?" Johnny strode toward C.J. and Shannon's heart thudded.

"Why are you always so quick to defend her? There's nothing in it for you if she wins." C.J.'s gaze bounced between Shannon and Johnny.

"Go find a cowboy your own size and gender to pick on." Johnny stared until C.J. backed off.

Shannon squeezed her hands into fists to keep from launching herself into Johnny's arms. She'd missed him terribly since her father had ordered him off the ranch two weeks ago. She needed to tell him how sorry she was that he'd been fired. Needed to tell him that she loved him. Instead, she said, "You came."

"Folks, Shannon Douglas is ready to ride! She's comin' out on Mr. Shorty, a bull from the Bob Evans ranch in Silver City, New Mexico."

Johnny checked Shannon's grip. "Mr. Shorty likes to turn to the right. Sit low and inside when he spins."

"For those of you who keep up with women's rough-stock events, you may have heard Shannon suffered a concussion and broken leg…"

The last thing she needed to hear before the gate opened was a recap of her wreck on Heat Miser. She willed Johnny to make eye contact with her, but his gaze remained on the rope. "How does your grip feel?"

"Good."

"Count to eight then—"

"Dismount on the right. I've been practicing just like you said."

"You're ready." He squeezed her hand, then dropped to the ground outside the chute.

Johnny's presence calmed her jittery nerves and Shannon focused her thoughts inward, determined not to disappoint him. She clamped down on her back teeth and nodded to the gateman.

Mr. Shorty did his thing—fast, quick bucks and tight spins. Her body felt the physical strain of the ride but her adrenaline gave her the strength to hold on. She ticked off the seconds in her head and when the buzzer sounded, she planted the heel of her right boot against Mr. Shorty's flank and shoved off. She landed several feet away from the bull, then sprang to her feet and dashed for the rails, ignoring the pain in her Achilles tendon.

"Folks, Shannon Douglas just showed us why she's one of the best female bull riders in the country."

The stands erupted in a boot-stomping jamboree as the JumboTron replayed Shannon's ride. She waved to the crowd and retreated behind the chutes where the TV cameras couldn't see. Her calf muscle burned as she took off her gear. She didn't care to stay and watch C.J.'s ride. She assumed he'd make it to eight on his bull. "Let's go," she said, grabbing her gear bag.

"He wants a word with you." Johnny nodded to a reporter standing off to the side.

"I can't."

"I'll take care of it."

That Shannon hadn't had to explain herself to Johnny confirmed all over again why she loved and admired him. When he came back, he took her gear and they went outside to his truck, which sat parked next to hers. "Grab your things," he said.

She didn't argue. She retrieved her overnight bag and hopped into the passenger seat of his vehicle.

"Where are you staying?" he asked.

"I didn't get a room." She hadn't wanted to jinx herself by assuming today's ride would be uneventful and she'd make the second go-round tomorrow.

"I've got a room at the Holiday Inn Express not too far from here."

That he'd made a hotel reservation proved his trip to

Tucson hadn't been a sudden decision. She wished she had the courage to ask why he'd come.

Shannon waited in the truck while Johnny went into the motel and checked in. Then he drove to the back of the building and parked. He stared her in the eye. "We're sharing a room."

She was afraid to read too much into his words. She'd find out soon enough why he'd come to Tucson.

He carried their bags into the motel and she did her best to disguise her limp. He stopped in the middle of the first-floor hallway and swiped the key card in the lock, then stepped back and allowed her to enter first.

Shannon noted the king-size bed as she made her way to the window. She cracked open the heavy drape, letting in a sliver of sunlight. Johnny set their bags on the floor and when their gazes met across the room, her heart melted and she longed to lose herself in his arms.

Her eyes locked with his as she unbuttoned her shirt. Next, she unbuckled her belt and pushed her jeans over her hips. The denim dropped to the floor. When she reached for the strap of her bra, Johnny moved so quickly her breath caught. His fingers caressed her shoulder before lowering the strap and baring one breast. Then he swung her into his arms and she clung to him.

In Johnny's embrace she was able to forget her fear and anxiety and rejoice in the feeling of sweet relief that she hadn't caved in to her fears and scratched today. Shannon was beginning to believe that with Johnny by her side, anything was possible.

"READY?" JOHNNY ASKED as he and Shannon stood in the cowboy ready area at the Tucson rodeo grounds. The need to touch her was strong, so he straightened her Kevlar vest and handed her the protective face mask.

They hadn't said more than a few sentences to each other since they'd woken at the motel several hours ago. He'd read the questions in her eyes… Why had he come to Tucson? What did it mean? He'd come because he couldn't stay away. Because whether Shannon rode bulls or not, he loved her and he wanted to be by her side no matter what happened, but now wasn't the time to discuss their relationship. His first priority was to make sure she remained safe.

Last night he'd prayed for the hours to slow to a crawl but damned if they hadn't flown by, leaving him standing next to the bull chute, experiencing a sense of déjà vu as Shannon prepared for her second ride against Rodriguez.

"Lightning Strikes bucks straight up," she said. "I can handle him."

"Yes, you can." The words sounded convincing, but Johnny had his doubts. Lightning Strikes was a three-time bucking bull of the year. Only seven cowboys had ever made it to the buzzer on him. The odds of Shannon lasting eight seconds weren't in her favor.

The announcer gave the crowd a brief description of the Dynasty Boots sponsored event and the history between Rodriguez and Shannon along with yesterday's results—both of them had made it to eight. Shannon and Rodriguez had each scored an eighty-four.

"We got ourselves a tie between cowgirl and cowboy. Let's see if Shannon Douglas edges out the competition today. The action is at chute five. This cowgirl is going head-to-head with Lightning Strikes!"

Johnny felt as helpless as a newborn baby—unable

to protect Shannon from whatever fate awaited her once the gate opened. "Stay low and dismount on the right."

She hopped onto Lightning Strikes and wrapped the bull rope around her hand. "Shannon." When she glanced at him, he said, "I'll be right here when you're done."

He backed away from the chute, worried that his hovering would make her more nervous. Besides, the bull had become antsy. The sooner the pair left the chute, the better. Shannon nodded to the rodeo helper and the gate opened. Lightning Strikes lunged for freedom. She stayed centered and low as she came out of the first spin. Johnny wanted to check the clock, but he couldn't look away from the action.

The bull continued to buck high and tight. Everything was going well until Shannon slipped sideways during a spin. The buzzer sounded, but Johnny didn't hear it, his eyes remained glued to Shannon. *C'mon, baby, you can do it. Find an opening.*

She dropped farther down the side of the bull.

What was she waiting for? *Now, Shannon, now!*

She attempted to move her leg into position, but the awkward angle of her body prevented her from pushing off and she fell straight to the ground, the bull's hooves missing her head by inches. Johnny's heart stopped beating as she attempted to roll away. The bull rotated in her direction and she aborted the effort, diving sideways to avoid getting stomped.

Move, baby, move!

As if Shannon heard his command, she scrambled to her feet and stumbled the first few steps before gaining her balance and running for safety as the bullfighters distracted Lightning Strikes.

She staggered like a drunken woman into the cowboy

ready area and removed her mask. Once she'd thanked the cowboys who congratulated her, Johnny held her trembling body close—so close he feared he'd suffocate her.

She'd survived round two.

One more to go.

SHANNON LEFT THE BED and escaped to the bathroom. As quietly as possible, she lifted the toilet seat and vomited—twice. There went the nice steak dinner Johnny had bought her to celebrate making it to the buzzer on Lightning Strikes.

Heaven help her, she was a disaster—both physically and emotionally. Her body was battered and bruised. Icing her Achilles tendon hadn't helped—her leg felt on fire. To be honest she'd never thought in a million years she'd be having this much trouble with the tendon and for the first time she was forced to consider that it might be a career-ending injury. She couldn't continue to be competitive unless her leg was a hundred percent, which meant if she didn't win tomorrow her run for the title might be over.

And it wasn't just her banged-up leg that would force her to retire her bull rope. As much as she wanted to believe she had control over her fear, the nightmare that had followed her home from the hospital had reared its ugly head tonight and she feared if she fell back asleep the visions would cripple her and prevent her from competing tomorrow.

After she flushed the toilet, she leaned against the tub and rested her head in her hands. Everything came down to one ride and she'd drawn the tougher bull. Smackdown—a bull with a reputation of turning on his riders. A bull that had yet to be ridden this year. A bull most cowboys yearned for the chance to conquer.

A bull capable of winning her the title.

A bull she wanted nothing to do with.

The look on Johnny's face when he learned which bull she'd drawn proved that he was scared for her, too. She was so grateful he'd come to Tucson to support her, yet she wished he hadn't come, because she knew she was putting him through hell.

Her stomach heaved again and she lurched toward the porcelain bowl. After she flushed the toilet she heard a noise in the other room and noticed a shadow beneath the door.

Was Johnny listening to her retch? Seconds passed and finally the shadow disappeared. Forcing her shaky legs to hold her, she stood and brushed her teeth before turning out the light and slipping into bed. She lay in the dark listening to Johnny breathe. After a few seconds he lifted his arm and she nestled her face against his neck. The smell of his faded cologne and male scent soothed her ragged nerves.

"Can I ask you a question?" Johnny's deep voice drifted into her ear.

No. "Sure."

"Why are you letting your mother have so much power over you?"

"What do you mean?"

He shifted on the mattress and faced her, his chest bumping her breasts. "Neither winning or losing the title will change the fact that your mother abandoned you."

"When I was little, I felt all alone and no matter how hard I tried to keep up with Matt and Luke and make my father proud, I didn't feel like I fully belonged with them."

"And you blamed your mother."

"I resented not having a mother to talk to about girl things." She tried to gather her thoughts but emotions got in the way. "My anger festered, which only made me more determined to be like my brothers and do guys things like rodeo."

"So you wanted to punish your mother."

Had she? "Rodeo gave me a focus and helped me forget that my mother wanted nothing to do with me." Rodeo was her life. All she'd ever done—it was who she'd become.

"Have you talked to your father about this?"

"He already blames himself for raising me like a tomboy."

"So winning the title is going to make you feel better about your mother leaving you and your brothers?"

Why did it sound immature when Johnny said it? "It'll make up for the pain of knowing my mother didn't love me."

Johnny threaded his fingers through her hair. "Try to get some sleep. I'm right here. I won't let anything hurt you."

She closed her eyes, trusting him to keep the nightmares at bay. As the first rays of sun peeked through the curtains, she drifted off to sleep and Johnny lay wide-awake.

He stared at the ceiling. It had torn him to pieces when he'd stood outside the bathroom door, listening to her vomit. Now that he knew what demon rode her back, he felt even more helpless, because there was nothing he could do to change Shannon's childhood or the fact that her mother had left the family.

He and Shannon shared similar childhoods and he felt a connection to her on a deeper level than he'd experienced with anyone else. He wished he was enough to fill the void left by her mother, but based on his own experience with abandonment issues, he'd learned that nothing he did or tried to do would make the pain go away.

Did she realize that her decision to compete today was putting him through hell and back?

This isn't about you.

Shannon was about to confront the biggest challenge of her life and she needed him—not to stop her, but to stand by her side and be there for her no matter what the outcome.

He swallowed hard when he thought of Smackdown—a badass nasty bull. Rodriguez had drawn Let's Party, a middle-of-the-road, straight-forward bucker. The cowboy would make it to eight, which guaranteed him a victory if Shannon got thrown.

Johnny resisted the urge to wake Shannon. He desperately wanted to make love to her, but feared that kind of closeness would break the promise he'd made to himself—that he wouldn't make her choose between him and rodeo. She wiggled against him and he kissed the top of her head. "You awake?"

"Mmm." She stretched her arms above her head, exposing her breasts when the sheet dropped. "I'm hungry."

So was he. Hungry to make love to her one more time.

"Let's eat a big breakfast," she said.

"We'll stop at the Waffle House on the way to the rodeo grounds."

They took turns getting ready in the bathroom, then

packed their overnight bags. "What's wrong?" she asked when he didn't walk to the door.

"I have something to say."

She dropped her bag. "Okay."

"I love you."

Her eyes rounded.

"I just needed you to know that before…" He closed the distance between them and held her by the shoulders. "I'm in love with you, Shannon. I started falling in love with you way back in August when we danced after the rodeo in Gila Bend, but I didn't realize the depth of my feelings until…" He'd watched her get run down by a bull.

She opened her mouth to speak, but he cut her off. "I want to spend the rest of my life with you."

"Johnny."

He was so damned rattled and worried about the rodeo that he was making a mess of his proposal. "This isn't the place—" he spread his arms wide "—I imagined asking you to marry me. I don't even have a ring for you."

"You don't have to do this." She grasped his hand. "Nothing's going to happen to me today."

"I'm not proposing to you because I think you'll get hurt."

"You mean you're not asking me to marry you, hoping I'll reconsider and scratch my ride?"

"No! I love you, Shannon, whether you ride today, tomorrow or next week."

"But you don't approve of me riding," she said.

"It's not that I don't approve. I just wish I could make up for what your mother robbed you of as a child." He tucked a strand of hair behind her ear. "But I can't give you back all the things you missed out on growing up without a mother."

Tears flooded her eyes.

"If you'll let me, I'll be the man standing by your side when that chute door opens and the man whose arms you walk into when the ride's over." He didn't know how else to express his love, so he kissed her.

After their long, slow kiss, she whispered, "I love you, too, Johnny. There's no other man I trust more with my heart than you."

"Then marry me," he said.

Her smile was shaky, but her voice was strong. "I'd be honored to become your wife."

Their kiss was desperate yet filled with hope. When they broke apart, he said, "Whatever the future holds for us, we're in this together. Don't ever forget that."

"LADIES AND GENTLEMEN, welcome to the…"

"Quit looking over there," Johnny said when Shannon glanced at the crowd gathering near C.J.

She and Johnny had arrived at the rodeo two hours ago and her nerves were tied in knots.

As the rodeo announcer recapped the competition between her and C.J., Shannon inched closer to Johnny, absorbing his strength. Since he'd proposed to her in the motel room and she'd accepted, she'd tried not to think too much about the future, because each time she did, she was tempted to walk away from her ride. Johnny had handed her a valid reason to call it quits yet he hadn't asked her to scratch from the event today. He was willing to stand by her no matter the outcome this afternoon and for that very reason she wanted to win.

She'd been uncertain about her future after today but

now that she knew she was spending the rest of her life with Johnny—no matter the result of today's ride—she planned to retire from rodeo.

"You ready, daughter?"

Shannon gasped. Her father and brothers walked toward her. Matt and Luke were grinning but her dad's expression remained sober.

"You came," she said.

"We've been here all weekend, Shannon, watching from the stands," Luke said.

Stunned, she couldn't find her voice. Johnny nodded to her brothers and they walked over to the stock pens, allowing Shannon and her father privacy.

"Daughter, I've been a lousy father to you all these years."

"That's not true."

"When you got serious about competing in roughstock events, I assumed if I showed my disapproval, you'd quit. But you're as stubborn as your old man and I'd raised you not to be a quitter, so I don't know why I thought you'd listen to me." He removed his hat and rubbed his brow. "No matter how tough you acted, you were still my little girl and the thought of you getting hurt... Honest to God, I didn't know how to handle my fear."

"Do you want me to scratch this afternoon?"

"No. You've worked hard for this moment. It's yours for the taking."

Shannon hugged her father. "I love you, Dad."

"We need to do that more often," he said.

"What's that?"

"Hug. I've missed hugging my little girl."

She swallowed the lump in her throat, then smiled when she noticed the Cash clan heading her way, Dixie leading the charge. Johnny's brothers all wished her well on her ride and then Dixie stepped forward and hugged her. "Go get 'em, girl."

"Johnny proposed to me," she whispered in Dixie's ear.

"Please tell me you said yes." Dixie squeezed Shannon's hand. "My brother is so in love with you, he's beside himself."

"I said yes."

"Good. We've always been like sisters, now it will be legal." Dixie nodded to the bull the rodeo helpers loaded into the chute. "We'll be here afterward, Shannon."

"I know." The love and support of Johnny's family and Shannon's best friend topped off an already emotional confession from her father. Right now…right here…she realized she had it all—everything that mattered most in life and her mother couldn't rob her of her happiness.

Everyone returned to the stands to watch Shannon's ride except Johnny—he remained with her behind the chutes. Gazing into his blue eyes she decided that she'd ride Smackdown—not to put C.J. in his place. Not for the childhood her mother had stolen from her. But for her and Johnny—to celebrate their unconditional love for each other.

C.J. rode first, the announcer making a big deal out of his career stats. The gate opened and the first three seconds of C.J.'s performance were textbook bull riding. Then he must have gotten cocky, because the bull bucked C.J. off his back. The arena sat in stunned silence.

"Well, folks, I sure didn't expect that from an experienced bull rider like Rodriguez. Looks like the ball is in Shannon Douglas's court. Will she make it to eight?"

Shannon eased onto Smackdown's back. The bull's

muscles bunched but he stood quietly while the rodeo helpers fished the rope from beneath him. The announcer rambled on about the grudge match between Shannon and C.J. The voices quieted in her head as she envisioned herself coming out of the chute.

Slowly, her fear and anxiety disappeared, replaced by the confidence she felt in the gift of Johnny's love. A future brighter than she'd dreamed possible lay ahead of her after the next eight seconds. She smiled at Johnny as adrenaline raced through her bloodstream like rocket fuel, then she nodded to the gateman.

Smackdown vaulted into the arena and executed a double kick before turning in a tight spin. Shannon had anticipated the move and stuck like glue to the animal's backside. The bull continued to spin but she hung on, fighting with every ounce of her strength. When the buzzer sounded the fans came to their feet, the noise rocking the arena. She remained alert, waiting for an opening to dismount.

The bullfighters ran at Smackdown and he stopped spinning. Shannon planted her right boot heel against the bull's side and pushed off with all her might. She landed on her chest, knocking the air from her lungs. As she struggled to her feet, she saw that the rodeo helpers had opened the gate for her escape and Johnny stood waiting. She stumbled once, then ran.

Shannon raced toward Johnny. Toward their future together.

And she never looked back.

* * * * *

Be sure to look for the next book by Marin Thomas in her new series, THE CASH BROTHERS! Available in October 2013.

REQUEST YOUR FREE BOOKS!

2 FREE NOVELS PLUS 2 FREE GIFTS!

LOVE, HOME & HAPPINESS

YES! Please send me 2 FREE Harlequin® American Romance® novels and my 2 FREE gifts (gifts are worth about $10). After receiving them, if I don't wish to receive any more books, I can return the shipping statement marked "cancel." If I don't cancel, I will receive 4 brand-new novels every month and be billed just $4.74 per book in the U.S. or $5.24 per book in Canada. That's a savings of at least 14% off the cover price! It's quite a bargain! Shipping and handling is just 50¢ per book in the U.S. and 75¢ per book in Canada.* I understand that accepting the 2 free books and gifts places me under no obligation to buy anything. I can always return a shipment and cancel at any time. Even if I never buy another book, the two free books and gifts are mine to keep forever.

154/354 HDN F4YN

Name	(PLEASE PRINT)

Address	Apt. #

City	State/Prov.	Zip/Postal Code

Signature (if under 18, a parent or guardian must sign)

Mail to the **Harlequin®** Reader Service:
IN U.S.A.: P.O. Box 1867, Buffalo, NY 14240-1867
IN CANADA: P.O. Box 609, Fort Erie, Ontario L2A 5X3

Want to try two free books from another line?
Call 1-800-873-8635 or visit www.ReaderService.com.

* Terms and prices subject to change without notice. Prices do not include applicable taxes. Sales tax applicable in N.Y. Canadian residents will be charged applicable taxes. Offer not valid in Quebec. This offer is limited to one order per household. Not valid for current subscribers to Harlequin American Romance books. All orders subject to credit approval. Credit or debit balances in a customer's account(s) may be offset by any other outstanding balance owed by or to the customer. Please allow 4 to 6 weeks for delivery. Offer available while quantities last.

Your Privacy—The Harlequin® Reader Service is committed to protecting your privacy. Our Privacy Policy is available online at www.ReaderService.com or upon request from the Harlequin Reader Service.

We make a portion of our mailing list available to reputable third parties that offer products we believe may interest you. If you prefer that we not exchange your name with third parties, or if you wish to clarify or modify your communication preferences, please visit us at www.ReaderService.com/consumerschoice or write to us at Harlequin Reader Service Preference Service, P.O. Box 9062, Buffalo, NY 14269. Include your complete name and address.

HARI3R

THE LONG, HOT TEXAS SUMMER
by Cathy Gillen Thacker

The second book in the McCABE HOMECOMING *series.*

Welcome back to Laramie County, Texas, where things are heating up between Justin McCabe and his new carpenter!

There were times for doing-it-yourself and times for not, Justin McCabe thought grimly, surveying the damage he had just inadvertently inflicted on a brand-new utility cabinet.

It was possible, of course, this could be fixed, without buying a whole new cabinet. If he knew what he was doing. Which he did not—a fact the five beloved ranch mutts, sitting quietly, cautiously watching his every move, seemed to realize, too.

A motor sounded in the lane.

Hoping it was the carpenter who was supposed to be there that morning, Justin walked to the door of Bunkhouse #1, just as a fancy red extended-cab Silverado pickup truck pulled up in front of the lodge. It had an equally elaborate travel trailer attached to the back. A lone woman was at the wheel.

"Great." Justin sighed as all the dogs darted out of the open door of the partially finished bunkhouse and raced, barking their heads off, toward her.

The lost tourist eased the window down and stuck her head out into the sweltering Texas heat. A straw hat with a sassily rolled brim perched on her head. Sunglasses shaded her eyes. But there was no disguising her beautiful face. With her sexy shoulders and incredibly buff bare arms, the interloper was, without a doubt, the most staggeringly beautiful female Justin had ever seen.

She smiled at the dogs. "Hey, poochies," she greeted them softly and melodically.

As entranced as he was, they simply sat down and stared.

She opened her door and stepped out. All six feet of her.

A double layer of red-and-white tank tops showcased her nice, full breasts and slender waist. A short denim skirt clung to her hips and showcased a pair of really fine legs. Her equally sexy feet were encased in a pair of red flip flops.

She took off her hat and shook out a mane of butterscotch hair that fell in soft waves past her shoulders. She turned and tossed the hat on the seat behind her, then reached down to pet his five rescue dogs in turn. The pack was thoroughly besotted.

Justin completely understood.

If there was such a thing as love at first sight—which he knew there wasn't—he'd be a goner.

THE LONG, HOT TEXAS SUMMER
by Cathy Gillen Thacker.
Available August 6, 2013,
from Harlequin® American Romance®.
And watch for two more books in the series this summer!

SADDLE UP AND READ 'EM!

Looking for another great Western read? Check out these August reads from the HOME & FAMILY category!

THE LONG, HOT TEXAS SUMMER by Cathy Gillen Thacker
McCabe Homecoming
Harlequin American Romance

HOME TO THE COWBOY by Amanda Renee
Harlequin American Romance

HIS FOREVER VALENTINE by Marie Ferrarella
Forever, Texas
Harlequin American Romance

THE MAVERICK'S SUMMER LOVE by Christyne Butler
Montana Mavericks
Harlequin Special Edition

*Look for these great Western reads AND MORE
available wherever books are sold or visit*
www.Harlequin.com/Westerns

American ★ Romance®

A Real Cowboy. A Real Home?

Rafe Rodriguez never reckoned on playing hero to a
beautiful, big-city stranger. But when he saves
Valentine Jones from a charging bull, this Rodriguez
brother's fate is all but sealed. The Hollywood
photographer is on location in Forever to scout out
an authentic dude ranch. And nothing could feel
more real—or right—than the fiery feelings Val's
awakening in Rafe. And he knows just how their
real-life romance should end!

His Forever Valentine
MARIE FERRARELLA

**Available August 6, 2013,
from Harlequin® American Romance®.**